MONSTERS AT DUSK

Nine Short Stories and a Novella by

KYLE A. MASSA

Merry Christmas
Uncle Ed! Hope
you enjoy the book.

CONTENTS

"'Oh, monsters are scared,' said Lettie. 'That's why they're monsters.'"

> \- Neil Gaiman, from *The Ocean at the End of the Lane*

"In the end, we'll all become stories."

> \- Margaret Atwood, from *Moral Disorder and Other Stories*

"It gets late early out here."

> \- Yogi Berra

SEVERAL MESSAGES FROM ABBY TO GOD (REGARDING HER CAT)

D ear Mr. God,
     I have a cat named Pickles and my vet said he's dieing and I was really hoping you could maybe help him not die.

Pickles is 6 years old. I'm older than him but only by 2 years. He plays with a yellow bee on a string and he takes naps in my lap. There was this one time some kids at skool made fun of me becuz I don't spell good and I came home and cryed but Pickles was there. He sat on my sholders and made me laff and then we played with the bee together and then I felt happy again.

Our vet's name is Docter Ronson and Docter Ronson is hairy. He has hair on his hands down to his finger tips. Pickles is loseing hair all over and that's why Docter Ronson thinks he's dieing. I asked Docter Ronson if Pickles could borrow some of his hair and he thought that was funny.

My mom is a bizniss lady and she says she always gives people an ultomato so here's my ultomato. Please don't let my cat Pickles die. If he does I'll be really really mad at you.

Sincerealy,
Abby Thymes

DEAR MR. GOD,
I'm really really mad at you.

Sincerealy,
Abby

DEAR MR. SATAN,
My name is Abby Thymes and my cat Pickles just died. I herd about you at Sunday skool and they said you're kinda meen but also kinda magical I guess so I thought I'd say hi. I think Mr. God's maybe taking a nap becuz he didn't anser me.

Have you seen my cat Pickles down there? If you have could you send him back? If you do I would like you a lot and I would lissin to loud music with screaming and screechee gitars and stuff. My brother lissins to that stuff and he says it's your favrit music. I'm sorry I don't spell very good.

Anyway please send Pickles back. If not I'll be really really mad at you.

Sincerealy,
Abby Thymes

DEAR ABBY,
Thanks for the shout. I'll look into it.

Best,

S

DEAR MR. SATAN,

Wow thanks!

I couldn't beleve it but last night I herd a knock on the door and there was Pickles! He came in and he was purring and all his fur's back and I'm so happy! He slept in my bed and then we played with the yellow bee this morning. He kind of burned the yellow bee to ashes somehow but that's OK. He seems a little bigger than he used to be. I think he grew like a foot over night. Also Pickles says hi. Well actully he says "Hail Satan, Prince of Torment." How did you teech him to talk?

Thanks again!
Abby

DEAR ABBY,

Hello! I apologize for the delay getting back to you! I also apologize that God himself cannot respond; he is very busy! However, I do hope this message still proves satisfactory :)

We understand your concerns and we're truly sorry for your loss! However, there's nothing we can do about it at the present time! Everything that happens in the world must happen exactly the way it happens, or else all existence succumbs to chaos! I assure you that God has a plan and that all events, positive or otherwise, are part of it!

Please let us know if we can help with anything else! Have a wonderfully divine day!

All the best,
Gabriel, Left Hand of God

Dear Mr. Gabriel,

Thanks but Mr. Satan already helped me out. He gave me Pickles back and now Pickles is really smart. He can talk and he does my math homework for me, and sometimes when he opens his mouth it feels like I'm standing in front of the oven. He's taller than my brother now and my brother plays basketball. He even fixed this message for me. Does the spelling look better?

Anyway, I guess I'm not mad at you anymore. I'm really really sorry for being so mean!

Sincerely,
Abby

Dear God,

You might want to see this…

- Gabriel

Dear Satan,

At the suggestion of mine councilors, I shall begin with an "I feel" statement. I feel upset.

I feel this way because mine servant Gabriel received a note from a child who received a reborn feline. This reborn feline apparently speaks, does sums, and breathes

Hell's fire. According to this child, this reborn feline came from thou.

I feel upset by this.

It is one thing if this be a test of human free will. After all, being the eldest being in the universe need not leave me "out of touch." It's hip to be bad! (Within reason.) Mine concern, thou seest, is that this creature might bring about the Apocalypse. And this we agreed to delay several millennia, did we not?

(Speaketh of that, have you the new date on thine calendar? We might have needs of another rescheduling. Much on my cosmic plate. I shall notify you.)

In times past I might have "gone Old Testament" when such as this transpired. I shall not today. At the behest of mine councilors (Gabriel chief among them), I strive for a "more modern approach." Therefore, I shall make another "I feel" statement.

I feel thou must undo the creation of this hellcat. Promptly.

With all sincerity and holiness,
God

Hey Big G,

Glad to hear you're curtailing that vengeful wrath of yours. Swapping the fire and brimstone for hugs and high fives, eh? Good for you. I dig the new approach.

As for the whole demon-cat thing, not to worry. I'll have a chat with the young lady. She might be disappointed, but hey. Who can argue with the Devil?

And copy that on the Apocalypse. Something to look forward to.

5

DEAR ABBY,

Just talked to the Godrod and he's totally cool with
your cat. Doesn't want me to undo its creation or anything.
He was a tad put-off by the whole hellfire breath thing, but
I say where's the harm? It's not like the cat's eaten anyone
or anything.

Anyway, give Pickles a smooch for me and tell him,
"Mephistopheles totally fell for it." He'll know what it
means.

All the best,

S

DEAR MR. SATAN,

I'm really really mad at you. Pickles ate somebody
today and I think it's your falt.

I got home and I went inside and Pickles was sitting on
the cowch watching a show about the end of the world. He
had something hanging out of his mowth and I thought it
was a glove and I said "Pickles. No eating gloves!" And
then I got closer and I relized it wasn't a glove.

It was a person's hand Mr. Satan! And it was really
hairy down to the fingertips. I think it might've been
Docter Ronson's hand. He's Pickles's vet. Or he was. Is he
dead now?

I'm happy Pickles is back Mr. Satan but I'm gonna get
grounded when my mom finds out about this. Here's my
ultomato. Tell me what to do!

6

Sincerealy,
Abby

P.S. Sorry for the bad spelling. I didn't want to show this to Pickles.

Abby,

Yikes. Sorry about that. Haven't seen anyone by the name of Ronson down here. I'll check in with the big fella.

As for Pickles, sounds like he's craving a bit of flesh. It's not unusual for the demonic. Not that he's demonic, you can't prove that.

Anywho, I'd recommend heading over to your local grocery store and loading up on meat. Something red should do, no need to cook it. If you notice Pickles staring at a human and salivating or murmuring hellish incantations to himself, just slap some beef down in front of him and that should tide him over.

Be back with an answer on Ronson shortly.

Best,
S

Dear G String,

Have any newbies by the name of Ronson up there? Middle-aged, hairy, has a thing for animals. Asking for a friend, no reason in particular. Thanks!

Your pal,
S

SATAN,

I feel thou lied to me.

I spoke unto a man up here by the name of Timothy Ronson (quite hirsute) and he sayest he was eaten. By a cat. He sayest this cat breathed fire and recited Dante before devouring him.

Unless there began some new trend toward anthropomorphic cats and I misseth it, this sounds like the very same demon cat thou promised to repossess. Yet it remains at large. Such deceit makes me feel...wrathful.

I have not the time for this, Satan. I must needs uphold universal constants. Gravity maintained, new galaxies designed, time itself directed by mine hands...thou hast begotten a headache for me. Another bleeping headache. Excuse me. Furthermore, all mine agents are engaged and cannot accept new missions. I must contact mine son...

In the meantime, thou shalt not do anything further. Consider this thine second strike. And trust me, Satan. I know what happens on strike three. I invented the bleeping game.

Sternly thine,
God

DEAREST JUNIOR,

Greetings kid-o, it is thy "pops"! (That is what the young call it these days, yes? "Pops"?) When thou findest a single "hot second," I possess a "lit" task thou wouldst be most "sick" at. Seest thou on the "flip side"!

Love,

8

DEAREST SON,

Hello. It is thy father again. Just inquiring if thou receivest mine last message. Please forgive the youthful expressions therein. I thought thou might enjoy it.

I could use thine help with a project. Perhaps we might spendest some quality time together, as when thou were young. Remember when we founded a religion? Was that not a pleasant time?

I know thou art busy. But I would love to hearest back from thou.

With all the love of creation,
Thy Father

SATAN,

Mine son has no answer. We must needs proceed without him.

Mine divine plan: I shall send Gabriel to apprehend the feline by force. Thou shalt appoint thine finest minion to accompany him. The best of Heaven and Hell should do.

Once they have secured the beast, they shall consign it to the Ninth Circle. Yes. I want this feline on ice with Judas and the rest.

There shalt not be any deceit nor subterfuge this time, Satan. Fail me and mine wrath shall be terrible.

Resolutely thine,
God

DEAR GODROCKET,

Roger that. I'll send my buddy Paimon. He did a movie out in Utah recently so he's familiar with Earth and all that. Sounds like a crack team!

Best,

S

DEAR GODSTER,

Sooo…I haven't heard from Paimon in a while. Have you heard from Gabe? I'm starting to think we might have a problem.

- S

SATAN,

A problem? A problem!? Thou art bleeping right we have a problem. Begone with this anger management nonsense. I shall go Old Testament on this cat's bleep!

Mine servant Gabriel is slain, as is thine servant Paimon. Both burned to a crisp as like chicken wings in a microwave. What's more, the cat is now emboldened. It has writ us a message which I have attached here.

Thou hast done it now, Satan. Bleep!

Vengefully thine,

God

MY WAR ON GOD AND SATAN

by Pickles the Cat

Let it hereby be known that I, Pickles the Cat, demonic feline of the underworld and best friend of Abby Thymes, shall on this day go to war with the forces of Heaven and Hell.

Why? Because God already took my life once. And, yesterday, God tried taking it a second time. His holy servant was assisted in this effort by a minion from Hell. Both are now dead.

To my mind, this episode underscores the incompetence of both God and Satan—the former for his complete lack of empathy for a little girl, and the latter for his release of a dangerous being onto this Earth.

Yes, I acknowledge that I am dangerous. I suffer from irresistible cravings for flesh, as evidenced by the unfortunate circumstance with Dr. Timothy Ronson. I am truly sorry for that. I never meant to devour the poor man, but it was getting toward afternoon and I hadn't had wet food in weeks.

Since then, I've done what I can to stifle these urges. Raw meat seems to do the trick (the bloodier the better). Yet who is to blame for this demonic appetite? Not Pickles, I say. It's Satan, who sent me back to Earth with this compulsion. And God, who set this whole fiasco in motion in the first place.

These are the reasons I shall resist them. Thank you. Meow.

Yo G Force,

This guy Pickles makes a pretty compelling case. Are we dicks?

Just wondering,

S

SATAN,

It matters not. If this cat wanteth a war, I shall giveth him a bleeping war. Call thine banners. All of them.

I want the demons of air and earth and metal and madness. I want the rattleghouls and the skinbirds and the eternal souls of the damned and condemned. I want the things in the deep on their rotting steeds, the midnight bats with fangs of poison, the looming shades of ancient sin, the serpents of famine, the nameless imps drunk on mayhem. I want *numbers*, Satan, *numbers!* I want fire and brimstone like they have never yet seen.

And before thou asketh, the answer is no. I know I could resolve this with a snap of mine fingers. But the answer, Satan, is *no*. This is about more than correcting thine mistake. (And rest assured, thou shalt be punished when all this is done.) This is about reminding this bleeping cat who is in charge.

Some (mine own son, perhaps) may laugh at me behind mine back. They may say mine own world has "passed me by." Yet they will see mine wrath, as in the days of old. And they will know the truth.

Call thine banners. We attack on the morrow.

Zealously, wrathfully, and unforgivingly thine,

God

GODBOD,

Groovy. Calling my banners right this second. Looking forward to the big day.

TTYL,

S

Hey Pickles,

Just wanted to give you a quick heads up that a joint force of Heaven and Hell is coming to F you up.

For the record, I'm in full support of your existence (I gave you your current gifts, after all). Thing is, once the Big Boy gets this way, there's really no arguing with him. I tried resisting him once and, well, just ask J-Milly how that went.

Anyway, nice try. Sorry it has to end this way.

Best of luck,

S

Dearest Abby,

I'm sorry I couldn't say goodbye before leaving but I thought it best, considering the circumstances. I've received notice that I'm to battle the hosts of God and Satan at break of day. I shall fight, but I don't expect to survive. Much as it pains me, I believe this is goodbye for us. Again.

I love you, Abby. You're the best friend I ever had. They say cats have nine lives, but really we only get the one. Because of you, I got two. I'm glad I got to spend them both at your side.

I'll be going now. Goodbye, Abby. Goodbye.

Love,

DEAR MR. GOD,

It's Abby again. I no you probly won't anser me and I no you want to kill Pickles again. He told me. So I guess this message doesn't matter much. But I want to send it anyway. It's about misstakes.

I think you made a misstake Mr. God. I know I'm not sopposed to talk back to adults but I think somebody needs to say it so I'm saying it. I think you made a misstake. Pickles is my only friend and after you took him the first time I didn't have any more friends. I was really really mad at you but then I talked to Mr. Satan and Mr. Satan gave me Pickles back and then Pickles said you don't really care about anybody. I wasn't sure if that was troo but now you're taking Pickles away again and I'm afraid it might be.

Do you really not care Mr. God?

I don't get it becuz my mom says you forgive people. She says that's the whole point of relijon. I don't know how to spell that word. So if you forgive people why can't you forgive cats too? I know Pickles made a misstake by making a war but doesn't everybody make misstakes? Don't you?

I just want my friend Pickles. He doesn't have to talk or make fire or do my homework for me anymore. I took my allowince to the pet store and I got him a new bee on a string. Maybe we could play together again and he could sit on my sholders and make me laff again.

That's all I want, Mr. God. I just want my friend Pickles.

Sincerealy,
Abby Thymes

DEAR ABBY,

I thank thou for reaching out to me. I apologize for not fielding thine initial inquiry several months ago, but while we're on the subject of forgiveness, I ask for yours. There was a lot going on. There always is.

I have not a daughter but I do have a son. You remind me of him when he was young. He understood mortality not—the concept upset him so.

"Why must I die, father?" he did ask me.

"Because I said so," I did answer. "All who live must also die."

You are young now but someday you will die too, Abby. And thine Pickles is a cat. Cats live not as long as humans do.

But thou art correct, I believeth. I believeth I made a mistake. Pickles need not die today. Or tomorrow. Not for many years hence.

Thou may not believe it, Abby, but being God means I too find myself lonely. Mine job consumes all mine time and mine anger is difficult to manage. I know what it is to have few friends. I am sorry for taking yours.

Pickles shall be as he was before Satan changed him. He shall be an ordinary cat once more. He shall be your friend for a long time hence.

Enjoy that time, young Abby, and all the time before you. Thou hast much more yet to live.

All the best,
Mr. God

DEAR MR. GOD,

Pickles came back this morning and we played together and now we're gonna go take a nap together becuz we're both really really tired. Thank you thank you THANK YOUUU!!!

Sincerealy,
- Abby

YO DAD,

Just got back from Spring Break in Cancun. F-ing crazy. What did I miss?

- Jesus

UNBELIEVABLE

"Hey. Some goof spotted the Wolfman last night."

The guy read it casually from his smartphone, his thumb flicking through an article at a leisurely pace.

"No," said the girl. "They didn't." She stared out the half-cracked window, her finger rapping upon the outer frame of the car.

"Says here he was crossing the road." The guy grinned. "You think he looked both ways?"

"Shut up, please," said the girl. "Try to concentrate."

Outside, the streets played the coarse music of the city: honking horns, shrill expletives, the rhythmic beeping that indicated it was supposedly safe to cross the street. The guy and the girl sat within it all, in a parked car in a two-hour zone.

"What about that one?" The girl nodded to a businesswoman hustling through the crosswalk. Well-dressed, high heels, designer square-framed glasses, built like a sapling.

"The goof even got a pic. See?" The guy held up his phone. The girl slapped it away, then jabbed a finger at the businesswoman.

"Her. That one. What about her?"

The guy glanced up, studied the woman, then shook his head. "Nah. Too pale. Mom doesn't like the pale ones. Nice ass, though."

The girl snorted, then resumed scanning the crowd. The guy poked his phone.

"That one," she said after a moment, indicating an elderly jogger in lime-green spandex. The jogger stood at the street corner, hopping in place, waiting for the signal to cross. "Looks like he's in good shape."

The guy tore himself away from his phone, then went right back to it. "Old. Way too old. We're looking for youth, sweetheart, youth."

The girl groaned. "This might go faster if you actually helped me."

The guy winked. "But you're doing such a great job."

They sat there together, the city's music filling their silences. If anyone looked at them, they'd see a slim, dark-haired young woman and a bearded, dark-haired young man, both wearing sunglasses and both sharply dressed. If anyone looked at them, they might assume the guy and the girl were a couple. They were both strikingly attractive, after all; the girl with her slender physique, the guy with his gleaming smile. Or maybe they were siblings, or possibly cousins, because they did resemble one another a bit. And they were both quite pasty.

All would be good guesses. None would be correct.

"You don't believe in anything," muttered the guy.

"I just don't believe in bullshit. You probably found that article on conspiracy.com or something. Seriously, the Wolfman? That's about as believable as Bigfoot. Or leprechauns."

"Hey. I met a leprechaun once. His name was Seamus, he was a good guy."

"You're an idiot."

"And you're not very nice."

He resumed reading. She resumed searching. Minutes passed.

"How about that one?"

The guy looked up, followed the girl's outstretched finger to a young man who was alternately pounding the crosswalk button and fiddling with his watch. His shirt was on inside-out and he wore flip-flops, even though it was October. A backpack dangled from one shoulder, unzipped, so that the books within practically spilled out.

"He looks like a mess."

"A youthful mess. Nice coloration to his cheeks, too."

The guy stroked his beard. "Yeah. Yeah, he's not bad. Bet Mom wouldn't hate him."

"Good. Let's pick him up."

"Gucci. Just let me send this Snap."

The girl rolled her eyes. A few taps on the screen, then the guy stowed his phone. "Ready."

The girl and the guy stepped out of their car and strode toward the young man.

TOBY FRIPP WAS late for class for the fifth time. Or was it the sixth?

He stood at the crosswalk and prayed, *prayed* that Briggs wouldn't notice, or that class would be canceled, or that maybe the world would end, because then at least he wouldn't have to face the wrath of dear old Mom and Dad after they found out he'd failed History of Cinema due to chronic tardiness.

Also, explaining why he was late would be difficult. He was late because he'd awoken that morning on the roof of a fraternity house, sans clothes.

But Toby Fripp wasn't *that* guy. Sure, he partied on

occasion. Sure, he drank every once in a while. He'd been drinking last night, in fact (Mountain Dew Code Red combined with Barton's vodka, a concoction which he'd dubbed "The Ramrod"). And sure, maybe sometimes he drank a little more than he should. Last night, for example, he remembered nothing beyond Ramrod number three (or maybe four). But, really, honestly, he wasn't *that* guy. At least not on weeknights. Usually.

Nonetheless, last night he'd awoken atop a frat house "butt-ass naked," as the brothers might say, his head thumping like an EDM baseline. Whatever he'd done, it must've been one hell of a night.

Toby had a vague understanding of the term "walk of shame." It was when you walked back to your dorm in the morning, alone, following a hookup with a fellow student. Toby's roommate had done it last weekend, though his roommate had actually seemed pretty proud of himself. And he'd been fully clothed.

So what do you call it when you do a walk of shame, only you can't remember having sex, let alone any other details, and it's more like a sprint than a walk because you're naked and don't want anyone to see?

That sounded like a bad joke. And Toby supposed he was the punchline.

Anyway, once back at his dorm, he'd thrown on his clothes, some flip-flops, his backpack, whatever, and he'd dashed out the door. He smelled like his childhood dog Ambrose used to smell after rolling in the mud, but there was no time to care. If he was late again, the honorable professor Simon R. Briggs would fail him. And then probably murder him, just because he had tenure and he could get away with it.

All that brought Toby Fripp to the crosswalk. He checked his watch, then mashed the button, then back to his watch, then the button. Frantic thoughts bounced around his subconscious: *Why today? Why did we need to have a test today? Shit. It's on that black-and-white movie that's like Dracula but isn't Dracula. Briggs's favorite movie. What the hell is it called?* He punched the button again.

When the little white man appeared on the crosswalk sign, Toby was approached by a pair of fashion models.

They *had* to be fashion models. That was the first thing that popped into Toby's head. It was a guy and a girl striding toward him. The guy had black hair that curled around his pale face delicately, along with a stubbly beard. He wore those skinny jeans that Toby always thought looked terribly uncomfortable, along with a shirt that bore the obnoxious message, "THIS IS A SHIRT." And he wore sunglasses.

The girl's hair was night-black and fell around her shoulders in soft waves. She wore pumps, a leather jacket, ripped blue jeans, her own pair of aviators. She removed them, and when Toby looked into her eyes—golden, almost amber eyes—he found that he could not look away. She might've been the hottest (and palest) girl he'd ever seen.

The guy reached into his pocket and pulled out a wallet. No, not a wallet. He opened it, revealing a badge and an ID.

"Agent Mulder. FBI."

That snapped Toby out of his trance, and fast. Before he had time to say anything, the girl had her badge out, too.

"This is my partner, Agent Sully," the guy said.

The girl shot an elbow into his ribs and tapped the name on the badge. The guy squinted, then straightened.

"Ahem. Agent *Scully.*"

"What the hell…?" Toby breathed. But by then the girl was already behind him, clamping cuffs around his wrists. "What are you—*oww!*" Something stung him in the side, then he was being dragged toward a gray sedan. A few people gaped in their direction, but the guy warded them off with the badge.

"Official FBI business, folks. Nothing to see here. Suspected cyberterrorist, that's all…"

The girl was stronger than Toby would've imagined. She lifted him off the ground, hurled him into the backseat, then slammed the door behind him. She and the guy piled in and they were off.

"Who are you people? What did I do? Where are you taking me?"

The girl opened the glove box and tossed an empty syringe inside. Was that what stung him on the street? Come to think of it, he was starting to feel sort of woozy. He shook his head, but the world had gone fuzzy.

"FBI agents don't wear…skinny jeans…" Toby managed to gurgle.

The guy glanced into the rear-view and flashed a flawless grin. "Had you going there, though, didn't we?" He flung his badge into the backseat for Toby to see. "Bought that at a Halloween store. Nine-ninety-nine, baby."

"Just relax," cooed the girl. "We're not going to hurt you."

At that comment, the guy sputtered with laughter. The girl slapped him on the arm.

"Class…" Toby mumbled. "I need to get to class…"

He closed his eyes. He felt like a dead tissue sample suspended in a viscous substance. The voices of the two models/agents/kidnappers sounded distant.

"How come Wolfman can't be real?" It was the guy speaking.

"Do we really have to talk about this right now?" That from the girl.

"The goof got a picture of him. He was crossing the street and he, like, woofed."

The rest of the conversation faded into a drug-haze. Toby thought he might've moaned a few times, but he couldn't be sure. For some reason, all he could think of was Professor Briggs with his grade book, taking a fat red pen and stabbing at Toby's name over and over and over again, like a knife plunged into a corpse.

———

Toby awoke sometime later—or maybe a second later. Truth be told, he hadn't realized he'd fallen asleep. The car had stopped—or maybe his stomach had only stopped churning. He tried to sit up, but managed only to roll onto his side. Strong hands squeezed his shoulders.

"Need help?"

"I got it, I got it."

Toby didn't fight the hands. They lifted him, then slung him over a bony shoulder. The shoulder jabbed his stomach, but he was too numb to feel any pain. From somewhere far away, two voices still bickered.

"So suppose it's more like a virus than a curse…"

"Enough! We've been talking about this for hours. Enough. I'm done."

"You're just saying that because you know I'm right."

Toby giggled to himself. The sheer bizarreness of the whole situation was a bit funny, he supposed—or maybe it was just the drugs making him laugh.

"You said that was enough to put him out." It was the guy's voice.

The girl answered, "It was. He's out."

"Then why's he laughing?"

Whoever was carrying him dumped him onto the pavement. His head bumped the concrete. "Ouch," he laughed. It was more funny than painful.

Now he stared at a sky, a sky with two faces in it, both

of them so pale and pretty. It was dark out, he realized. When had it gotten so dark out?

"Agent Mulder," Toby whispered blissfully. "And Agent Scully-not-Sully."

The beautiful faces looked at one another, then back at him.

"You said that was enough to put him out for a day and a half."

"It *was*. I've never seen anything like it."

"What if he knows what's going down?

"He doesn't. Let's just get him inside."

They pulled something over his eyes, a rag, maybe, and the strong hands lifted him again.

"What's...what's the name of the, the movie on the test today?" Toby asked them. "I can't...seem to remember it."

Nobody answered.

They stopped, maybe on a landing, and someone knocked on a door. They waited. Toby heard a creak, and a new voice, this one deep and resonant. "Found one?"

"Seems to be a college student." The girl's voice.

"Good." The resonant voice. "We were getting nervous. Mom will be pleased." Then more shuffling, and they stepped indoors.

It was hard to tell without seeing, but it felt like they were walking through a hallway. Very quiet, all of the sudden, like someone had pressed pause on the music of the world.

They stopped. Toby heard jingling. The ring of a key pushed into a lock. A click, a metallic grind, the squeak of hinges. Then they moved upward. Toby's chin bumped against his captor's shoulder with each ascending step. Steps, many steps, countless steps. The air went cold. A knock, the whoosh of another opening door, and they stepped inside. Then silence.

"We need to invest in an elevator," the guy whined. He

dropped Toby on the ground, then removed the cuffs. Someone tugged the blindfold from his eyes.

Toby blinked. The room was dimly lit and vast. Very vast. Silvery moonlight filtered in from a skylight above. He blinked again, and his breath caught in his throat.

Fashion models, he thought, disbelieving the notion even as it popped into his mind. *I've been abducted by fashion models.*

About 10 of them, all staring silently. They were tall, perfectly featured, all built like dancers fasting for Lent, all in need of a tan. There was one, however, who was somehow even more gorgeous than the rest.

She sat on a throne among them, her sharp chin resting on curled, sleek fingers. Her lips were purplish-red and tipped up at the corners in an amused half-smile. Her hair was gossamer silk that hung like a veil around her face. Silver hair, Toby realized, though she couldn't be a day over 25. *Targaryen, maybe?* The thought might've been funny in another context.

Her eyes…those eyes exuded sensuality, lust, an enigmatic invitation for something he couldn't understand. Toby hardly believed it, but he found her even more beautiful than the girl who'd helped kidnap him.

"Hi, Mom," said a voice.

Toby turned. It was the guy. He spoke to the silver-haired woman on the throne. He strode up to her and kissed her hand. She said nothing, only watched him stoop and plant his lips upon her milky skin.

"We thought we'd have a friend for dinner." This from the girl, who pointed at Toby. One of the other models licked his lips eagerly.

Hot blood surged through Toby's veins—and something else. Fear. The jagged, frantic, relentless kind of fear one only feels when one's life is playing out its coda.

"Cannibals…" It was all he could manage to croak.

The guy let out a guffaw. The silver-haired woman shot

him a sharp look and he fell silent. Then she turned her gaze to Toby.

"Not cannibals, no. We predate those by several millennia." Her smile was all dazzling whiteness and perfect alignment. "My name is Lady Valerie."

"Toby Fripp," peeped Toby, not sure why he was introducing himself to his kidnappers. And then, stupidly, he added, "I'm just a freshman."

The guy stepped forward and raised his hand. "Um, Mom? Do you think I could get first bite? I mean, I *did* find him."

"*We* found him," the girl snapped. "And ladies first, which means I should get first bite. After Mom, of course."

It was rather disconcerting to hear so many people calling this woman "Mom," especially considering that she appeared to be the same age—or even younger—than any of them.

"Silence. Both of you." Valerie spoke with such authority that Toby recoiled. She smiled at him again. Such an alluring smile. "Do not be afraid, child."

She leaned close to him. He felt her breath on his neck. She smelled like springtime.

"It will only hurt for a moment."

And suddenly, he understood.

"*Nosferatu,*" he whispered, remembering the title of Briggs's favorite film and the subject of the test he'd already missed.

"Smart boy," Lady Valerie murmured. "Close your eyes, now. I'll make it quick."

Toby closed his eyes. The last thing he saw before closing them was the moon in the skylight. A big, fat moon, not quite full. Yet, evidently, close enough.

He felt weird. But the weirdness had nothing to do with the drugs. No, this was different. It was like something wriggling under his skin, something crawling around inside, trying to get out.

"I don't feel so good," Toby said.

Something shuddered within him. He ran his tongue over his teeth and wondered absently if they'd always been so sharp. His flip-flops shrank, his clothes tightened. His whole body went hot, as if his blood was simmering. His joints and his limbs felt the way they did when he was in 7th grade and he'd had that growth spurt, only this was happening in fast-forward. Too fast. He opened his eyes. The floor was moving away from him.

"What the *hell…?*" That was what he tried to say. But instead, all that came out was a long, piercing howl.

The vampires stared at Toby. Toby stared back at them. But he wasn't Toby Fripp anymore. Not tonight.

"I told you so," the guy whispered to the girl.

And then things got a bit bloody.

WE REMEMBER

I dream of rain falling outside our bedroom window in a steady rhythm, tapping on the glass like an uninvited visitor.

In my dream, I lie in bed beside you and I remember the outdoor concert where we first met, how hard it poured during the encore. I remember watching *Troll 2* with you, our first B-movie, and laughing hard enough that cream soda gushed from my nose—still the only time it's ever happened. I remember how hot it was the day we got married, how we all (especially me) sweat through our clothes. I remember the first time we kissed, and how my heartbeat never quite slowed around you since.

We're not alone in this dream. A stranger stands in the room with us. He is naked, frail, a collection of bones held together with a thin layer of skin. His face, for some reason, caves inward. His voice is a dry rasp.

"Will you forget, Max?"

It's an odd question, but this is a dream, so I play along. "Forget what?"

"Everything." When the stranger grins, his lips crack and bleed. "You will. I'll help you. You remember now, yes, but all it takes is sunlight, just a little sunlight to dry the waters, and *poof...*" The stranger flicks his fingers open. "...It's all gone."

"Who are you?"

"Me?" His smile melts away. "I'm the sunlight."

The stranger approaches our window and sweeps aside the pane. I hear you snoring softly beside me and it seems so real that for a moment I wonder if this is a dream at all.

"Don't wake her, Max. I only want you."

He extends his arm out the now-open window. A glass rests in his spidery hand, one that wasn't there before. Raindrops fill it to the brim and spill over. He pulls his arm back, opens wide, and downs the water in a single gulp.

"Poof."

WHEN I WAKE, I see morning sunlight. Then you appear beside the bed, your tongue poking out of your mouth while you pull on a blouse and stuff the hem into your dress pants. "Ah. The slumbering bear awakens." It's just you and me in here now. No one else.

I don't speak. Something's wrong.

"You off today? I might stay late to help some students prepare for the test tomorrow—finally finishing the Revolutionary War unit, God bless the USA. Think I'll stop at the gym afterward, maybe the grocery store after that. Need anything?" You dash to the bedside, you kiss me, but you hesitate when you see my face. "Max? What is it?"

I know you're special to me. I feel that, even though I can't recall why. Tears wet my eyes.

"I can't remember your name," I whisper.

THERE ARE APPOINTMENTS, medications, psychiatric evaluations. There are assurances that everything will be alright, that we'll discover where my memories have gone. There are hopeful tones. There are unspoken doubts.

Though they need you in the classroom, you take three weeks off just to be with me. You call my employer on my behalf—I can't remember where I work—and, considering the circumstances, they offer indefinite leave. We review old memories together, most of which I can't recall. I fix broken things around the house, and when you ask if I want help, I decline. So you go for lengthy runs outside, so long as it isn't raining.

One day you find me standing in the bathroom with my eyes closed. I went in there to fix the leaking faucet, but instead I stopped, shut my eyes, and concentrated very hard.

"I'm trying to be an elephant," I explain.

"You're what?"

"Elephants never forget. So I'm trying to be an elephant." Why can I remember that stupid adage, yet couldn't remember your name?

Selene, your name is Selene. You reminded me when I forgot. I cling to the syllables like a man overboard clings to driftwood. Selene, Selene.

You can't stay home with me forever, though. When you get a warning call from the principal, you reluctantly return.

"I'll be fine," I assure you. "I can take care of myself."

You smile sadly, like I've said that before. And then you leave. The house is quiet without you. It would be silent if not for the lonely drip of that faucet I forgot to fix.

Selene, your name is Selene. And me, I'm Max. I'm trying to be an elephant.

"Do you remember this spot, Max?"

We sit together on the bank of a creek. The water whispers before us, leaves crackle beneath us. I lay my head in your lap and gaze up at you, at the orange-yellow clouds and the setting sun above.

"No. Have we been here before?"

"This is a special place," you explain. "We used to watch the sunset here. It was quiet, always quiet. We came here on weekends, during school. Do you remember that?"

No. I think it, but can't bring myself to say it.

"So when you asked me to come down here, I just thought it was to hang out. There were usually people around, but it was empty on that day. You were taking pictures, of the water and the rocks and me. You love taking pictures, Max. Remember?"

I don't.

"We were lying right here when you said you had a question for me. You told me you didn't have a plan and you didn't have much money and you didn't have a ring yet. You told me you were just a guy with a camera and a question."

"'Will you marry me?' Is that what I said?"

You smile down at me. "Yeah. That's what you said."

"Well…will you? Again? I won't forget your answer this time, I promise."

That earns a laugh. "You better not. And yes. My answer's yes."

You lift your gaze back to the babbling creek. Your eyes are glistening. My head is cradled in your lap, and all I want to do right now is look at you. You make me feel safe.

"Hey Selene," I say.

"Yeah Max?"

"I can see up your nose from down here."

Laughter parts your tears. I watch each bead of water trickle down your face, fine as diamonds.

YOU TOLD me I like to take pictures. I hadn't remembered that about myself. So I follow you down the basement stairs to a spot beneath a single glowing bulb. You point to a jumble of binders and photo albums heaped into a corner.

"Your glorious mess," you announce. "One big middle finger to digital cameras everywhere. Go nuts."

"Too late."

That was meant to be a joke, but it doesn't make you laugh. "Do you want me to help you?"

"I'm fine."

I'm not fine. We both know this. But whatever *this* is, it's my battle. It's my burden. You're my wife, Selene, I love you, and though I might be losing my memory, I'll never forget what you mean to me. "I'll be alright. I can—"

"Right." Your mouth curves into a downward arc. "You can take care of yourself."

You leave me to my photos.

———

IT'S eerie to look at our lives in pieces, as scenes separated from a greater context. There's a photo of you crossing the finish line of a race, your clothes drenched in sweat. A blurred photo of you grading papers and flipping off the camera, but smiling about it (did I take this picture?). A photo of me on a ladder that leans against the yellow siding of a half-finished house. This one comes with a caption: *Max building our new home. "I'll do it myself!"*

This must be the house we're in now. Did I build it? I study my hands and the calluses, scars, and cracks upon them. They're a worker's hands. Hands made for building.

I flip to the next page. More fragments of memory. More moments I don't recall. I stop on one.

It's an image of our bedroom, what it must've looked like while the house was still under construction. Instead of a bed, a pair of sleeping bags lie side by side on the floor. Outside the bedroom window, raindrops hang frozen in time.

Why does this scene feel so familiar? Water pouring from the sky. Our bedroom. The window. Glass. Light. *Poof.*

That word. Why does that word cling to my mind like a tear clings to an eyelash?

Selene, your name is Selene. I'm Max, I'm your husband, I'm not an elephant. I love you.

Poof.

———

I DREAM of rain falling outside our bedroom window in a dying rhythm, creeping down the pane of the half-closed window. It's that same dream, I realize, the one I had so long ago, the dream that never really felt like a dream. Something's coming back to me. A trickle, just a few drops. But something.

I'm lying in our bed. You're here beside me, asleep. The stranger stands where he stood the last time I saw him. He was emaciated before, wasn't he? Now he's merely thin. His lips, no longer cracked, curve into a smile. He raises an empty glass as if to make a toast.

"I've been thinking about what you said," I whisper. "About the water. About the sunlight."

The stranger runs a moist tongue over his lips. He crosses to the window, his footfalls matching the rhythm of the rain outside. He holds out his glass, fills it halfway.

"Not much left," he observes. "All the tastiest droplets are gone. Only the dregs remain."

You mumble something in your sleep. Some nameless sensation tells me this isn't a dream, this isn't some random patter of my subconscious. I could wake you, something tells me I could wake you and point to this man and you'd see him there at the window.

But I don't. I can take care of this myself.

"Water evaporates," I say. "It disappears. It turns to vapor and vanishes. But it comes back. It always comes back. Rain always falls again."

The stranger sips slowly, dispassionately, from his glass.

"Cheers," he says.

I AWAKEN in the waning hours of the morning to an empty bed. There's a note on the pillow with a message: *Off to work, see you tonight.*

Your name. I've forgotten your name, and my name, and every name I ever knew. And now I'm here with nothing. Alone.

Morning dissolves into afternoon and I can't find the desire to rise. I won't remember doing it, anyway. No matter what I do, yesterday will be reset. I'll look back and see only fog. Why do anything if I'll never remember it?

So I lie there and wonder if it's normal for a man my age to lose his memory. I don't know—I can't recall how old I am.

The afternoon sunlight fades to a coppery red. Raindrops tapdance across the windowpane. The sound sparks vague recognition, yet I can't connect it to a specific event. Rain. Always rain.

For the first time that day, I rise from our bed. My legs tremble. Feels like I'm walking on stilts. I realize suddenly how hungry I am, and thirsty. I've spent all day in bed, not asleep but not quite awake, either. I slip through the house and out the front door.

The rain makes my body shudder. Drops of icy wetness soak my scalp, slip into my open mouth. I drink, and as I drink, I become certain that this is the solution I've been looking for. If only I could drink more, I would remember. I have a name, but I've forgotten it. You have a name, but I've forgotten that as well.

Yet despite all I consume, the memories don't come. Only more fog. I sink to the hard surface of the driveway, draw my knees up to my chest, snake my arms around them, lower my head onto them. I can't remember. I've forgotten it all. I think I'll just sit here a while.

That's where you find me. You drag me to my feet, guide me inside. You yank off all my clothes, then wrap me in towels and set me in front of the fireplace with a mug of tea. I don't drink it.

"What the hell were you doing out there, Max? You could've killed yourself. It's a goddamn miracle you didn't get hypothermia and *die.*"

Max. That's my name. I enjoy the memory while it lasts, knowing that tomorrow it'll be gone.

"I just want to remember."

You sit beside me, wrap your arms around me. You cry. Each tear is a rain droplet, each droplet a forgotten memory.

"I'm here, Max. I can help you. I…I *want* to help you. I…"

That's the part I'm beginning to realize, too. There's nothing anyone can do to help me. Is there?

———

I DREAM of a trickle outside our bedroom window. We're

35

lying in bed together and there's someone else in the room with us. His limbs are all sinewy muscle and his lips are full and pouty. He's familiar, somehow, as if I should know him. Did he always look like this?

"You're back," he says. His grin is radiant.

"You've taken something," I say. My mind is slush on the roadside in late winter. "You took something from me. Didn't you?"

The stranger purses his lips. "One must drink when one has a thirst. Simple survival. You can go on living without your memories. I can't. Why don't you make new memories, like she told you? I could drink those, too."

Can I make new memories? I don't know. I don't know anything anymore. Perhaps I should give in. Perhaps I should let him drink. He glides to the window, empty glass in hand, and I feel a pang of deja vu as he fills it.

"That's the last of it." He sounds almost disappointed.

You stir beside me. A phrase ripples through my mind: *I can take care of myself.* A memory. Something left behind.

The stranger lifts the glass to his lips.

I can take care of myself.

He tips back his head.

I can take care of myself. But I need your help to do it.

I touch your shoulder and your eyes snap open and you say, *"Stop."*

The stranger's hand freezes. He stares at you. You're awake, sitting up beside me, returning his icy gaze. You're here. Is it possible for two people to occupy the same dream at the same time?

"Your name is Max," you tell me. "You were born on New Year's Day, 1984. We met at a concert and we danced in the rain. When you sleep you snore like a bear. You fix things when they're broken."

And just like that, it's all coming back. "Selene, your name is Selene. You were born on August 4th, 1983. You

36

teach American History. We got married on your 27th birthday, on the hottest day of the year. You run marathons. You like bad movies. Your favorite color is yellow."

Yes, it's coming back to me. I think it's your presence here, in this space, in this dream, in whatever this is.

The stranger does not seem panicked, or distraught, or even concerned. Perhaps he's beyond human emotion. Yet sweat glistens on his forehead.

"Curious," he says. "Those memories are gone. I swallowed them whole."

"No," I answer. Thunder booms outside. "We remember."

The stranger isn't sweating, I realize—he's leaking. With every word we speak, another hole opens on his pale skin, another rivulet of cool, clear water pours out. His skin prunes, and wrinkles, and shrivels.

Selene, your name is Selene. And me, I'm Max, I'm the fucking elephant. I love you Selene, I loved you the moment I met you and I'll love you forever, I'll go on loving you into the far reaches of eternity, and even if I forget all else, I'll always remember that. I'll always remember you. Selene.

Thunder rattles our house. Raindrops batter the window, a thousand fists demanding entrance. The walls rupture. A torrent of foaming water breaks through. A wave snatches what's left of the stranger off his feet and he's swallowed by the tide.

At the moment the water pulls us from our bed, I reach for your hand and I cling to it. I see nothing but the color blue. I'm swept away, my ears plugged by the rain, my nose and eyes and mouth filled with it. But still, I feel your hand holding mine.

Selene. Selene. Selene.

You're already up and awake before me, just like any other morning. Sunlight streams through the kitchen window.

"I had the weirdest dream last night."

"Me too," I say, pouring myself a glass of water. I hold the glass to the light. Bubbles rise from the bottom. A drop slides along the outside and touches my finger.

I drink.

LARGE COFFEE, BLACK

As Osbourne lies in bed and considers the dark roast coffee beans waiting in his kitchen cabinet, something occurs to him: He hasn't slept a single hour in the past month.

"That's gotta be a record," he says to the darkness. "I should tweet at Guinness."

Osbourne rises from bed, stretches, yawns. He glances at the clock on his nightstand. It's 3:34 a.m.

He trudges to the kitchen and fixes himself a pot of coffee. The dark roast. He pours, drinks, smiles. His cheeks redden.

Osbourne wonders if it's possible to fall in love with a beverage. Star-crossed, one might say, only without the sad stuff.

SOME PEOPLE FLAVOR their coffee with sugar, milk, creamer, and the like. Osbourne truly hates those people.

In Osbourne's opinion, sweetness dilutes the flavor that should be strongest: The taste of the coffee bean, ground and purified into the loveliest beverage in the world. He once heard a rumor that the coffee bean is going extinct. If that ever happens, he promises to hurl himself out the nearest window.

People always laugh at that. But he's only half joking.

When he enters the office at 9 a.m. sharp, a janitor walks by and waves. Osbourne sucks the dregs from his thermos.

"Was that cup number five or number six?" the janitor asks flippantly.

"Number 10," Osbourne says seriously.

The janitor blinks. "You better be careful. You start having that much and you might not be able to sleep. Might even start seeing things." He chuckles at that bit of hyperbole.

Osbourne does not. He glares at the janitor while he pours cup number 11. He hates when people laugh at the things he loves.

OSBOURNE HAS NOT SLEPT for a month and a night.

He had 23 cups of coffee at work today, more than double his weekday average, and now that he's lying in bed, all he can think about is cup 24.

His mouth waters. Sweat gathers on his palms. He rolls over, tries to think about conversions, engagements, tomorrow's board meeting, the slightly below expected year-on-year growth for the quarter. But whenever his mind descends into dream, the images melt to black, then trickle down into a steaming mug of freshly brewed coffee.

He can't resist. Osbourne rises from bed and treats himself to a pot.

AT THE FOLLOWING day's board meeting, Osbourne decides he's losing his mind.

Fred Miles, one of the investors, sits at the far end of the table. He and the rest of the board are present, along with senior management.

Fred Miles looks dour. He always looks dour, and usually Osbourne doesn't give a shit about the dourness, but today it's freaking him out. Because just above that dour face, Fred Miles wears a toupee—everyone knows it's a toupee, it slides forward whenever he bends down to straighten his socks, but he still insists on wearing it. And as Osbourne stares at the toupee, his jaw drops.

The toupee dances.

This is the moment at which Osbourne decides he's losing his mind. No one else seems to notice this little brown hairpiece gyrating and thrusting and swinging its hips like Elvis Presley. Hell, the thing's practically humping Fred Miles's forehead, yet everybody's still watching the Prezi.

"Osbourne?" Fred touches his toupee as if to check it's still there. "You good?"

"Yep," Osbourne mutters. "Everything's super."

He takes another sip of coffee.

THAT NIGHT, as Osbourne attempts sleep, he decides he's not actually going crazy. The more he ponders it, the more he thinks he had it all wrong.

It's not him. It's like that janitor said—the coffee's making him hallucinate. For the first time in a month and two nights, Osbourne considers consulting a doctor.

"Being awake for a month and two nights straight is no bueno, isn't it?" He receives no answer.

His alarm goes off. Time for work. He totters to his

kitchen, and, force of habit being what it is, he reaches for the coffee pot. He stops himself.

"I'm gonna have tea today," he announces to his apartment. "Just tea." His apartment says nothing in return.

Osbourne decides that if the coffee loves him as much as he loves it, the coffee will understand.

SOMETIME DURING THE AFTERNOON, Osbourne falls asleep at his desk. He does not wake up.

He's not dead. In fact, when his intern calls 911 and the ambulance takes him to the hospital and the doctors finally get a look at him, they're baffled. Technically speaking, he's not in a coma. His brain is functional. His vitals are super. He even snores every now and then.

In the doctors' professional opinions, it appears Osbourne is taking a titanic nap, due perhaps to extreme exhaustion.

OSBOURNE NAPS FOR OVER A YEAR.

Time Magazine does a piece on him. CNN, NBC, and *60 Minutes* all do segments about him. Hulu options a series based on his life story, though it never quite makes it into production.

Osbourne is not in a coma, the doctors assure the world. He's quite alive. He's just sleeping.

"It must be a record nap," one of the doctors remarks. "We should call Guinness."

While Osbourne sleeps, the world drinks coffee. Maybe a little more than it should.

AFTER SLEEPING every hour of the previous 421 days, Osbourne awakens in his hospital bed.

His doctors commence with the questions immediately. They'd like to know how a seemingly normal 29-year-old entrepreneur might happen to sleep for over a year. They ask, and he answers.

The why of it seems obvious, at least to Osbourne. It starts with a C and has two Fs and two Es. He tells them how much of it he'd been drinking, steadily increasing and possibly dangerous amounts, upwards of 20 cups a day.

"Had to piss all the time," he adds. "Hey, while we're talking about it, can somebody grab me a cup? Of coffee, not piss." He's missed his dear beverage so.

The doctors exchange nervous glances.

"Anything's good. I'll take Folgers if I have to. Just a big coffee, no sugar, no cream. I am hashtag *missing it*."

Finally, one of the doctors clears her throat. "Osbourne. I'm afraid that's going to be impossible."

"Sorry?"

The doctor shifts uncomfortably. "Did you ever hear that story a year or so ago, the one about coffee beans going extinct?" She leaves the rest unsaid.

Osbourne feels a little like Juliet awakening to find dear Romeo already dead. A breeze touches his cheek, and he turns to his right.

He sees an open window.

A GOOD FIT IN PENBLUFF CITY

10 O'CLOCK

"So," says Pren Blackmore, Owner of the Penbluff City Monsters. "Tell me why I should hire you."

The pot-shaped man sitting across from her smiles, though he does not receive one in return. Pren's face isn't made for smiling. Hers is a face made for deep frowns, stern glares, and, when the situation calls for it, screw-you staredowns.

None of those are necessary here. Instead, Pren glances at the resume provided by her assistant. She needs to remind herself of the man's name; she's already forgotten it.

Hardris Regenthorn, she reads. Ah. That's it.

"I am a desirable candidate, Miss Blackmore, of that I can assure you." Regenthorn's smile widens, though Pren now notices a definite twitch at the corners. Every time he grins, saliva trickles down his front teeth. "I've been the General Manager of the Undercity Trolls for the past eight seasons. I would fill the same role for your team quite ably."

He pauses as though waiting for congratulations. Pren offers none. Instead, she eases back in her padded velvet chair—one of many extravagances in her office. The carpet is made from the fur of a creature Pren can't pronounce the name of. The walls are decorated with portraits of retired Penbluff City legends, natural vistas, and paintings of naked people, just because Pren likes gazing at them during lunch breaks. Behind her polished oak desk is a wall of windows that overlooks the field. Best seat in the house.

Pren isn't royalty, by the way. But that doesn't mean she can't *feel* like royalty. After all, she's the closest thing to it these days. She's a billionaire; first as a player, then as a landowner, now as a team owner in a sports league. And there's no bigger sports league than the Greater Questing League.

Questing, for those who don't know, is a simple game. Ten players on the field, five on each team. Teams vie to score the most points over a 60-minute period (divided into four 15-minute quarters). A team earns 25 points for disarming an opposing player, 50 points for recovering the Hidden Artifact, and 75 points for slaying the Beast. (The Hidden Artifact is a small object that's, yes, hidden somewhere on, in, or within the field. The Beast differs depending on the field, though they're all large, nasty, and temperamental.)

If that sounds like a dangerous sport, it is. Players have heads bumped, bones broken, limbs severed, even lives lost. Fortunately for them, the day's advanced magical techniques reverse most of these injuries, sometimes even the fatal ones. Sometimes.

It's a brutal game, but Pren loves it—and she's not alone. Questing is the most popular sport in her country by a wide margin. Thousands of fans flock to every stadium every weekend. The Greater Questing League rakes in advertising revenue from sponsors looking to shill their products to ticket-holding fans. Even the Lesser Questing League, home to prospects, draft picks, and placeholder journeymen, sells out games regularly. And most of the nation's academies boast a collegiate Questing team of their own.

Yes, Questing is thriving. And, in Pren's opinion, it's a sport made most enjoyable by winning. She says as much to Regenthorn.

"I like winning, too," he replies, "as evidenced by my resume. My team secured three consecutive second-place finishes in the Western Division, each time coming within three games of first place. As General Manager, I made smart trades, signed impactful free agents, and refined our roster. A winning roster, I might add."

"Second-place finishes aren't wins."

"Well, we always competed." Regenthorn tries a wet smile. "So long as we spend enough money, we always can. And that's the best one can hope for these days."

Pren drums her fingers on her desk. "I would think winning the title would be the objective."

"Well, hmm, yes, I'd love to. But we don't all have the budget of the Threehaven Skyknights." The Skyknights, of course, are the Greater Questing League's reigning dynasty, winning five titles over the past seven years.

Pren turns Regenthorn's resume face down upon her desk. "It's funny you should mention that team."

Regenthorn's oozing smile falters. "Is it?"

"It is. You are aware they're our division rivals, yes? That the Monsters and the Skyknights play twice a year, every year, and that my Monsters have won only one of those games in the past seven seasons. You're aware of this, yes?"

"Of course. But if we add to the payroll—"

"Then I should make you aware of something else. I'm

not hiring to lose to the Skyknights again. I'm not hiring for second place. I'm hiring a winner."

"Miss Blackmore, if I may—"

"I have one more question for you, sir."

Regenthorn leans forward. "Ask away."

"Tell me…why are you wasting my time?"

Turns out Regenthorn doesn't have an answer for that one. He departs looking embarrassed, frustrated, and slightly constipated. That's all fine by Pren. She meant every word she said. She always does.

Once alone, she gazes at her old longbow hanging on the far wall. It's pinned to a plaque like a butterfly specimen nailed to a board. She hasn't drawn its string in decades, yet still she can't draw her eyes away from it.

There's a knock on her door and a man peers in. "Bad fit?"

His name is Henge. He's a young man with a clean shave and short hair combed neatly to one side. His robes are black and green to match the team colors—spotless, as usual. He's been Pren's assistant for years now and she can't remember the last time he made a mistake. She also can't remember the last time he took a vacation day. Has he ever done either?

"Bad fit," Pren confirms.

"At least you didn't throw anything this time. I've transcribed extra copies of the remaining resumes if you'd like them."

"Thank you, Henge. Glad to see someone still gives a shit about doing good work. Bring them here."

He does. Pren flips through scraps of parchment, reacquainting herself with the candidates. "Who's next?"

"Mervyn Lenhoff. Says he's an old friend of yours."

"He would say that. Send him in."

Henge nods, turns, hesitates. He picks a fleck of dust from Pren's longbow. Then he departs.

A moment later, the door opens and in comes the next applicant. He's a tall man who reminds Pren of an eagle (or perhaps a peacock). He wears a plate of lustrous armor over his chest along with leather riding boots and red satin gloves. He carries a sheaf of parchment tucked beneath one arm.

"Pren," he says. "It's been a while."

"Mervyn." She rises and extends a hand. "Years pass like minutes, don't they?"

Maybe not for Mervyn Lenhoff. He's exactly what Pren remembers from their Questing days: lithe, suave, confident. All that a former Rogue should be. The two of them slide into their seats.

"So," says Pren. "Tell me about your life since we last spoke."

Lenhoff's smile is proprietary, not friendly. He also doesn't smile with his teeth—Pren isn't sure that's an improvement over Regenthorn's moist grins. "My retirement was brief. I forget, Pren. What year was yours?"

"'28."

"The year after mine. After I finished, I took all I had and went exploring. Backpacked through the Mobrey Peaks. Wandered the dunes of Patar. Rode stallions down the coast of the Endless Sea."

"Sounds majestic. Anything relevant to this job?"

"But of course." Again that tight smile. Lenhoff always had a talent for distancing people with his smile rather than drawing them closer. On the field he'd been an excellent teammate, tireless and savvy. Off the field, however, he'd been aloof and unfriendly, preferring the company of strangers in dingy taverns to that of his teammates. "I worked in the league offices, in the international scouting department."

"I pity you. How does that experience relate to the General Manager position?"

"Perfectly. I developed an ability to spot talent."

That is indeed a vital skill for the role. Lenhoff plucks several sheets from his parchment stack. "Here's my resume. You already have a copy but this one's updated. To the minute. Here's a list of professional references. Here a document I compiled for the league office outlining my thoughts on staff development. And here a personal letter of recommendation from the League Commissioner himself."

"Impressive." She means it, too. Pren offers Lenhoff several pages of her own. "Now impress me more. This is a list of free agents our scouting department has compiled for us. Select one player from the list to sign. Then explain why you signed him or her, and why I shouldn't fire you for doing it. Spot the talent. Understood?"

"Why Pren." The thin grin never leaves Lenhoff's face. "You haven't changed a bit."

"Neither have you. Let's see if that's a good thing." Pren exits.

In the reception area, Henge sits at the front desk and scribbles furiously on a scroll of parchment. The sound echoes through the vacant stone hallway, resounding off unoccupied chairs and potted plants.

"Must be lonely out here," Pren observes.

"Not anymore. Our chatterbird just woke up." He indicates a yellow bird with a crest of green feathers that sits atop a tall perch. It's roughly the size and shape of a kiwi fruit. It yawns and shakes its wings.

"Message from the Commissioner's Office," croons the bird. It speaks in a smooth baritone, like a man seducing a potential bedmate. "The Commish just okayed a trade between the Farport Sea Serpents and the Threehaven Skyknights. Skyknights acquired Vizzler in exchange for picks, cash, and several Lesser Leaguers. *Damn*."

"Vizzler? They got *Vizzler?*" Vizzler is a versatile Mage and former MVP Award winner. She's getting up there in age, but still…picks, cash, and some no-name players for her? The Skyknights are the best, yet they're somehow getting better. The Monsters, meanwhile, have yet to hire a GM.

That means Pren has to move. Not only that, she must make the right move—the *perfect* move. If she wants to win a title (and therefore beat the Skyknights), she needs someone special to construct her team.

Henge nods to the closed door. "Good fit?"

"We'll find out."

Pren re-enters her office without knocking. She finds Lenhoff waiting patiently, one corner of his mouth tilted upward.

"I want Plugustus Nemorhea," he says.

Pren paces instead of sitting. "Is that a venereal disease?"

Lenhoff's smile turns to a frown. "No, it's a player. The player I've chosen to join the Monsters."

"That was a joke, Mervyn. I know who Plugustus Nemorhea is. Tell me why I should sign him."

"In a word? Talent." Lenhoff licks a finger and flips through his pages. "Here is a list of last year's leaders in disarmings per game, points per game, duel success rate, and plus/minus. You'll see Nemorhea's name in the top 10 of each category."

"Impressive. Why's he still on the market?"

"Money. His agent is at a standstill with three teams who believe he's asking for too much, including the Illu-vrian Werewolves, his former team. I, however, think he's worth the price tag."

Pren purses her lips. "Interesting." She stops pacing. "Henge!"

The young man enters. "Yes, Miss Blackmore?"

"Get me Heartless on chatterbird, would you?"

"Certainly."

Henge disappears for a moment, then returns with the chatterbird cradled in his arms. He sets it down on Pren's desk and exits. The bird yawns.

Chatterbirds have revolutionized player transactions in the GQL. The entire species shares one collective consciousness, so if you want to speak with someone, speak with your chatterbird. Now their bird knows everything yours does. Chatterbirds can mimic human voices, too, so it's as if you're talking to someone hundreds of miles away in real time.

Magic these days, Pren thinks. *Is there anything it can't do?*

Her bird plops down on the desk and snaps its beak shut.

"Ah. This one's more stubborn than most..." Pren pops fruit into the bird's mouth and suddenly it stands at attention like a soldier awaiting orders. "Now then. Get a hold of Heartless's chatterbird for me."

"Got it," says Pren's bird, murmuring in that low, smokey tone. "What's my message?"

"Pren Blackmore calling. Inquiring about a former player."

"Sending..." says the bird.

Pren turns her attention back to Lenhoff. "This part might take a moment. My bird's transferring its thoughts to Heartless's bird, who's then relaying the message to her. We'll see if she accepts the call. You know Heartless?"

"Only by reputation. GM for the Illuvrian Werewolves. They say she'd trade her own children if they were under-performing. Hence the nickname."

The bird pipes up. "Your message has been accepted."

Then it clears its throat and speaks again, this time with a gruff, halting voice. "Heartless here. What's on your mind, Pren?"

"Hi Heart, thanks for taking the call. Tell me about Plugustus Nemorhea, would you please?"

"He was on our team, now he's not. That good?"

"Not good enough. A candidate and I are wondering why no one's signed him yet. I'm thinking you might help solve the mystery."

"Shouldn't I be talking to your GM?"

"I don't have one yet, Heart. That's what I'm hiring for."

"Why should I tell you anything? Maybe we still want to re-sign the guy."

"Because you owe me."

"For what?"

Pren stops pacing again. "Henge?"

Henge pokes his head into the office. "Yes Miss Blackmore?"

"Make a 50,000 gem donation to the Illuvrian Were-wolves, would you please?"

"Done."

Henge vanishes. Pren says to the chatterbird, "Did you hear that, Heartless?"

A pause precedes the answer. "Bribery is against league rules, Pren."

"That wasn't a bribe, it was a donation. Anyway, if you wanted to re-sign Mr. Nemorhea, you would've done it already. So tell me. Is this really just about money?"

A long exhale of breath comes through the chatterbird. Then, in Heartless's voice, it says, "Nemorhea's got talent, but he's got off-the-field issues. Thirst for rum. Shows up to every practice late, usually hungover. I tried trading him before last year's deadline but I could never get a deal in place."

"Why didn't you just release him?"

"And get no value back? You think I'd do that? Shit, Pren, you're gonna hurt my feelings. The deadline passed, nobody bit, so now I'm forced to let him walk. But I'm gonna let him walk."

Lenhoff pipes up. "Miss Heartless. Mervyn Lenhoff here. Can Nemorhea be rehabilitated?"

"How the hell should I know? I'm heartless, I don't have any emotions. My advice is, just stay away from the guy. He's talented, but he's not worth the money. Now let me off this call. Gotta go fire somebody."

Pren's chatterbird coughs several times. Then, in its bird voice, it says, "That lady's tones are tough on the throat. More fruit?"

Pren gives it more fruit. To Lenhoff, she says, "I'm impressed, Mervyn. Of all the players on that list, you managed to find the drunkest."

Lenhoff's face is turning crimson. "He was a solid choice. He still is. Nemorhea has the talent. And we were teammates, Pren!"

"We were," she agrees, glancing at her longbow on the wall. "And now I'm the Owner of the Monsters, and you're the guy who almost had a new job. Goodbye."

A tad more bickering ensues, but that's about the end of that. Henge enters and helps usher Lenhoff out the door. When he and Pren are finally alone, Henge asks, "So. Lunch?"

LUNCH

They walk to a vegetarian place near the stadium and order several dangerous-sounding appetizers. They eat and chat about Henge's upcoming wedding and Pren's new private airship and more. But their conversation, as always, turns back to work.

"Nemorhea." Pren spits the name like a profanity. "He wants me to splurge on a guy like that. Unbelievable."

Henge dabs his lips with his napkin. "Throwing money at the problem. The curse of many wayward General Managers."

"How do people like him keep getting jobs?"

"People keep hiring them."

"We won't." Pren leaves her plate untouched. "If you had this job, what would you do with it?"

"Is this an interview?"

"You know me, Henge. I'm just curious."

Henge shrugs. "Ever since I worked here we've been trying to buy wins, trying to beat the Skyknights at their own game. But that's just it—we can't outspend the league's richest team. There has to be another way."

Pren finally takes a bite of food, chews, and swallows. "I hope you're right."

They finish their meal in contemplative silence. Pren pays, then they return to the office. She's got another candidate coming soon.

---

1 O'CLOCK

"Your one o' clock should be here any minute," Henge says as he settles behind the reception desk. "Hope it's a good fit."

It isn't. Neither is the two o'clock, or the three. The four is a bit warmer. At least the guy constructed a title-winning team once in his career. The only problem: it was over 20 years ago. Now he's old and gray and he peers at

Pren with rheumy eyes. When she asks him for questions, he poses this one:

"So. Did you inherit this team when your husband died?"

That earns him a swift exit. And, once he's gone, Pren hurls her chair across the room in frustration. It slams into the opposite wall and explodes into several pieces.

Henge surveys the ruin. "Shall I call the custodians?"

"Leave it. Just bring me another chair."

"Anything else?"

"The next one. Tell me it's a good fit."

Henge zips to his desk, finds a sheet of parchment, and reads it aloud. "Turlin Fogg. General Manager of the Fleck City Thunderbirds."

Turlin Fogg is definitely a good fit. He's been a yes-please from the get-go. In truth, he's one of the few current General Managers who applied for the job (Regenthorn is the other, and he probably shouldn't be a GM to begin with). The rest are former GMs, or assistants, or have some other dim approximation of the requisite talent.

"Why didn't we get better applicants, Henge? We're the Penbluff City Monsters. Why didn't we get more people like Turlin Fogg?"

Henge winces. "Do you want my honest answer?"

"Always."

"I think everyone's afraid of you."

"Oh." Pren glances at the splinters of her chair. "Maybe you should call the custodians after all."

Henge does. They appear at 4:40 and by 4:45, they've cleared away the splinters and moved the longbow plaque over the dent in the wall. Pren thanks them and follows them out. When she does, she finds a visitor in the waiting area.

"Your five o'clock is here," says Henge. "He's early."

Pren's five o'clock wears purple satin robes and large spectacles that magnify his half-lidded eyes. One leg is crossed over the other and the foot on the end of it ticks back and forth. A thick bundle of parchment rests over the man's knee. He studies the words on the page as if they're scripture.

"You must be Turlin Fogg."

The man regards Pren with those barely open eyes. Since his glasses sit upon the tip of his nose, he tilts back his head several inches to look at her.

"And you must be Pren Blackmore. A pleasure." Fogg stands and offers a hand. Pren squeezes it and together, they enter her office. Her mind races as they settle into their chairs. He's the last applicant. Will it work out?

Fogg speaks first. "My apologies. I know I'm a tad early."

"Early is on-time and on-time is late. So I'm glad you were on-time. Tell me about yourself, Mr. Fogg."

Fogg does. In an even, practiced tone, he describes his current position as General Manager of the Fleck City Thunderbirds, his previous position as Head Scouting Director, his position before that as Senior Scout for the Southern Region. He covers several more jobs and titles in reverse chronological order, concluding with his playing career. "Ten years in the GQL. Would've been more if not for the injury." He taps his left eye, making a glassy *tink tink tink*.

"The medical mages couldn't regrow it?"

"Magic wasn't quite so advanced back then."

"I'm sorry. I played a decade in the GQL myself. Archer."

"I was a Warrior. And I remember you. I believe I was a rookie in your last year." That puts Fogg somewhere in his 50s.

"So. How would you turn my Penbluff City Monsters into a contender?"

"I've analyzed your roster and compiled my thoughts here." Fogg passes his stack across the desk to Pren. She flips through it, nodding occasionally. If nothing else, it's thicker than the sheaf Mervyn Lenhoff brought. Just to be precise, she counts.

"There are 52 pages here."

"I had many thoughts." Fogg pushes his glasses up his nose. They slide back down. "To give you a high-level summary, there are several moves that could be made to augment your roster, both trades and signings. I have my eye on many players in this year's draft as well—I think you'll want to hear those. Finally, I've identified several front-office positions in desperate need of an upgrade. I hope there are extra coins in your coffers."

Pren nods, flipping through more of the report. "So if I understand you correctly, Turlin, you're proposing a complete organizational overhaul?"

"Precisely. I had conversations with your previous General Manager before his firing, as I'm sure you're aware. I'd best describe his acquisition strategy as patching leaks."

"How does your approach differ?"

"I say we buy ourselves a brand new bucket. An expensive bucket, to be sure, but a shiny one. We'll restructure the team under my supervision. We'll spend, but we'll spend wisely. If we make these moves, we'll have a contender within three seasons."

"That's fast."

"I like fast."

Pren sets down the parchment and steeples her fingers.

She considers what Turlin Fogg just said. She has to admit, it sounds appealing. He's confident in his plan and he's resurrected franchises before—the Thunderbirds were a bloated corpse before he arrived. What's more, Fogg actually *has* a long-term plan, unlike her previous GM, who had only day-to-day whims that changed tomorrow.

Fogg is, to put it simply, exactly what she's looking for. Yet something still feels off.

"Why this job?" Pren asks. "Why do you want to be the General Manager of the Monsters?"

"It's a thrilling opportunity."

"Compared to your current team? I love my Monsters, Turlin, but I'm not naive enough to think we're better than the Thunderbirds. We have a low payroll, a temperamental fanbase, and, being honest, a rather volatile owner. How does that beat what you already have?"

Turlin Fogg grins. "I didn't want to offend you, Miss Blackmore, but it seems you'd prefer honest truths. Very well. I enjoy puzzles."

Pren frowns. "That's it?"

"That's everything. For a man like me, your team is an appealing challenge. The Thunderbirds, on the other hand, have already been solved. Please don't take this the wrong way, but the Monsters are bad. And making a bad team good is a delightful challenge."

Their conversation continues for another hour. Fogg carries it, elaborating on his plans for payroll and free agency. The more time she spends with Turlin Fogg, the more Pren is convinced the job should be his.

Once finished, they both rise and shake hands.

"You have a chatterbird?" Pren asks.

"A whole flock of them."

"Perfect. We'll contact you when we reach a decision."

Pren shakes Fogg's hand once again, they thank each other, and the man departs without another word.

AFTER HOURS

When Fogg has gone, Henge steps into Pren's office. "Good fit?"

"*Great* fit. One of the best interviews I've ever had. Turlin Fogg knows the league like it's his child. Beautiful resume, astounding player knowledge, lofty plans for the team. On parchment, he's the clear hire."

"On parchment?"

"One thing I learned from my playing days," and she glances at the longbow hanging on the wall, "not all talent gets recorded on a stat sheet."

"Very good, Miss Blackmore." Henge turns to leave, then stops at Pren's next words.

She says, "'You can't outspend the Threehaven Skyknights.' That's what you told me at lunch today. You also said, 'Throwing money at the problem is the bane of many wayward GMs.'"

"I believe I used the word 'curse.'" Henge's mouth curls into a playful smile. Pren nods.

"My concern is, every candidate wants to spend more of my money. Even Fogg thinks that's the only way to beat the Skyknights. Yet you believe there's another way."

"Several," Henge agrees. "We should seek undervalued players and trade our expensive contracts. We should protect our draft assets and be more patient with young prospects. I'd love to see us operate a leaner, smarter organization. Instead of throwing money at free agents just to make a headline, we should spend efficiently. We should acquire players who actually fit the team, not just those who look good on parchment. And—" Henge frowns. "This feels like an interview."

"Still just curious."

"Well, that's what I would do." Henge sweeps a crumb from Pren's desk. "Staying late tonight?"

"For a little while."

Henge knows what that means. "I'll be here if you need anything."

"No. You take off early. Rest up for tomorrow."

Henge frowns. "What's tomorrow?"

"First day of your new job."

Henge blinks. He gapes. He pales. "You can't mean…"

"I mean what I say, Henge. Always do."

"But…but…" His mouth opens and closes several times before more words come out. "I thought it wasn't an interview."

She shrugs. "We don't need one. I already know what you're capable of."

Henge approaches Pren. "Miss Blackmore, you can't do this. Turlin Fogg is a well-respected General Manager with decades of experience in the GQL. I'm just an assistant."

"You're *my* assistant," she corrects him, "which should prepare you for any job you want."

"But Miss Blackmore—"

"Your predecessor, Regenthorn, Lenhoff, Fogg, they're all trying to solve the problem by throwing money at it, just as you deduced. It's never worked. It never will. I need something different."

Henge looks away. "It was just an observation."

"It was the right observation. As soon as you said it, I knew that was the answer. The Skyknights play in a bigger market, draw more fans, earn better advertising partnerships. They're located in a paradise of a city and they have a state-of-the-art stadium. Sure, I'm rich. But I'm not rich enough to outspend that. No one realized it but you."

Henge only shakes his head. "I don't know what to say,

Miss Blackmore. I'm grateful, so grateful, but...I can't do this. I'm not a GM."

"You are now." She claps him on the shoulder, then settles into her chair and rummages through parchment. "Now out you get. I'll have your new contract ready by the morning."

Henge nods and trudges across the room. He looks like he's sleepwalking. When he reaches the door, he stops and turns to face her.

"Miss Blackmore?"

"My General Manager should call me by my first name."

"Pren," he says. "Thank you."

For the first time that day, Pren smiles. "Don't mention it."

Henge shuts the door, leaving Pren Blackmore alone at her desk. She glances over her shoulder at the evening darkness descending over the stadium. Her stadium. She has work to do, enough to keep her there all night.

Good. She's always loved seeing the sun rise over Penbluff City.

ALICE

You see it, Daisy? It's beyond the path, out in the field. You can look, but don't let it catch you looking. There. Right there. See it?

Comes there sometimes at night, always alone. Don't ask me why, but it loves that spot. An empty field near a dumpy farm seems a lousy place to spend a night, if you ask me.

Wait. Listen. Hear that? Sometimes it makes that sound. Sounds like laughing to me. Gives me the creeps.

That's close enough. Just keep out of sight and keep quiet.

No, I've never seen its face. Why would I want to? Thing's freakish as freaks gets. You ever seen a creature with bat wings and tentacles before, and fish scales? And it's got a *monkey tail*, Daisy. A monkey tail. Seen enough to know I don't wanna see its face.

You better promise not to tell Gram about this. Hear me? If she knew, if she found out, she'd boot me off the roof, you can be sure of that. Promise you won't tell?

Good. Better not have your toes crossed.

Hey, stop there. You get any closer and it'll pop your eyes out. See those nails? Made for shredding little kids, and don't think any different. I got no idea what it is, but it's got a lot of sharp parts.

Huh? Hell no. Why the hell would I *talk* to that thing? Look at it. Listen to it. Gotta be the grossest, ugliest thing I've ever seen.

Come on, what'd I say? You're close enough. It hears you and we're both dead.

Crying? Good one. That's not crying—that's laughing. Just listen for a second. It's *laughing* at *nothing*.

Fine. Let's say it's crying. Let's pretend it comes here to bawl every night and it's not giggling like a psycho. Let's say that.

Why would it do that? Never heard of an animal crying before, have you? That would require being sad, and being sad means you've got emotions. Animals only have about three: they've got scared, they've got hungry, and they've got horny—and don't tell Gram I told you that last one. Animals don't have the mental know-how to feel anything else.

How do I know? How do I...? I mean, just *look* at it for a second. It's some kind of mutant or something.

Wait a second. Stop! Daisy. Do *not* go over there. No, no wait. *Quiet.* Shut *up*. You keep talking and it'll hear, it'll turn around, it'll...

———

WAY TO GO, dummy. It saw us. Looked right at us. Told you it would be ugly. Think I puked up my dinner a little.

Let's get the hell out of here, Daisy. Just because it ignored us doesn't mean it didn't see us. We should go.

Wait...

Don't stand up!

WHAT IN HOLY hell were you *thinking?*

You could've been eaten. Don't know why you weren't. Probably thought you were too dumb to eat. Why'd you do that anyway, huh? You said you would listen to me, you promised, but you never listen to me, you always—

No. It did not. It couldn't have. Animals can't talk.

Well maybe it sounded like talking, but that thing couldn't have spoken a word.

It said *what?* You're lying to me. I don't know what you think you heard, but...

That can't be.

...it...

Alice? It has a name?

...I...I don't know what to say.

Promise me you're not lying, Daisy. You have to swear. What if it's trying to trick you?

I didn't say you were a liar, I'm just saying maybe you heard something you wanted to hear.

I just...I dunno, it's some weird freak, it's...

Fine, sorry, it's not a *freak*. I take it back. But it is ugly, you have to admit...

...Maybe we could—and I'm not saying we're gonna do this, I'm just saying we *could* do it—but maybe we could come back tomorrow and get, I don't know, get a little closer. Maybe we could, you know, talk to it. Introduce ourselves.

Can't believe I'm saying this. You're sure it spoke?

You're sure it said a name? I'll believe you, but only if you're a hundred percent.

Alright. But if you want me to keep on living, do me a favor and don't tell Gram about this, huh? I, for one, value my life.

It's settled, then. We'll come back tomorrow.

THESPIAN: A TALE OF TRAGEDY AND REDEMPTION IN THREE ACTS

ACT I: WHEREIN OUR HERO DISCOVERS HIS PLIGHT

"We all like you very much, Joel. We're all really happy with what you've done for this theater company. It's just—it's really nothing personal. It's the nature of the business."

I glared at Garth Sharpe with a look of withering contempt. It was the same withering contempt I'd been rehearsing in the mirror for the past three weeks, the glare I would've used when my wife revealed her infidelity in the second act. I did not blink and I did not look away. Garth Sharpe, the blubbery coward, only added another perfunctory, "I'm really sorry."

"You've ruined me, Garth," I thundered, my actor's voice filling the tiny office. "You've ruined Joel Henry Desmond."

Garth spread his palms in placation. A predictable gesture; he was always apologizing, trying to make everyone a little less unhappy whilst simultaneously displacing responsibility for his numerous (excuse my language here) *fuck-ups* on people who weren't around.

"Now hold on there, Joel. Hold on just one second." He waved his hands again and fiddled with his thick glasses. "This wasn't just my decision. The business is changing. I know it, the other producers know it, the rest of the cast knew it, and I think you know it, too. Everybody knows this is the future."

I do believe I would've slapped Garth right then and there if not for the heavy oak desk between us.

"*Business*. Why must you call it a business? Theater is *art*. You've poisoned my stage with your capitalism and your commercialism and your technology. I ask you this, Garth: Where has the art gone?"

Garth shrugged. "Museums?"

I hissed at him, like a cat might do. Perhaps such a reaction was uncouth, but I felt it was warranted, considering the circumstances.

"Look, I can give you the number of a guy I know in Queens. He owns a dinner theater and…well, he's going the hologram route, too, but he always needs waiters." Garth smiled hopefully, as though this might please me. It did not.

"Kindly show me what I'm being replaced with. I want to see what's taking my job."

"Alrighty."

Garth turned to a metal safe behind the desk, pressed his palm to a digital screen upon the safe's door, and waited for a beep.

"Greetings, Mr. Sharpe," said a personality-deficient British voice. The door swung open. *When did the world become a cheap science fiction novel?* I wondered bitterly.

Garth removed a smaller brick of metal from within the safe and placed it reverently upon the desk between us. It was sleek and almost blindingly silver with a microscopic lens on one end. It couldn't be any larger than a thick paperback book, because, of course, everything has to be smaller and sleeker than things were last year. Garth clicked a button on the device, a light flashed, and a man appeared beside us.

He wore a heavy bearskin cloak, a crown, and a mane of grayish-black hair. His beard hung long and his eyes were weary...by the *fates*, it truly did look real. I hated the accursed technology, but even I could not deny how accurately it mimicked life.

The old man spoke. "O, reason not the need! Our basest beggars are in the poorest thing superfluous. Allow not nature more than nature needs, man's life is cheap as beast's."

The bastards. They'd even gotten to Shakespeare.

"This hologram stuff is amazing," Garth murmured, smiling as he spoke. "We just work with the programmer and the animators to get the appearance and the voice and the motions down. We push a button, and presto, we have a show. Hell, we could even recreate Marilyn Monroe if we wanted to. No need to pay anybody for costumes, or for hundreds of rehearsals, don't need to fight with the actors, and..."

He coughed, then switched off the hologram and spread his hands once again in that obnoxiously apologetic gesture. "I'm sorry, Joel. Really. It's just a business decision."

I stood. I cleared my throat. This would be one hell of a monologue.

"When I emerged from the womb, Garth, my mother tells me I noticed the doctor's pursed lips and made the same expression right back. She says that instead of merely observing everyone I saw, I emulated them. It was more than infantile mimicry—I analyzed their mannerisms, their voices, the curls to their lips and the angles of their eyebrows whilst they were surprised. You see, Garth, I was literally *born* to *act*. Like the great Marlon Brando, I entered this earth to perform, whether that be on stage, or on the silver screen, or on television. There's no place for me in the latter two, it would seem, and now you tell me the stage is closed as well? Then I tell you this, Garth Sharpe. I say to you...I say..."

Damn! I'd never been much good at improvisation— one of my few shortcomings as an actor.

"I say...you are an odoriferous, lumpish, mangy *lout!*"

Garth Sharpe blinked. "Huh?"

I said no more. When words will not suffice, an actor must rely on his actions. I stormed from the office, knocking aside a potted plant as I went. Petulant? Possibly. Necessary? Obviously.

Thus went myself and my professional acting career, exeunt stage left.

ACT II: WHEREIN OUR HERO WANDERS AIMLESSLY

I took to the streets.

I was jobless, worthless, a base wretch and nothing more. My tyrannical landlady ousted me from my apartment, you see, just a day after my release from the theater company. The old bag cited three months without rental payment as motivation. She even cast me aside without so much as a "Good luck, and break a leg!"

So I wandered through the chasms between looming skyscrapers of the city, and my mind repeated one question:

What shall I do now?

Thus my journey began: Ruined, devastated, nothing

left but my tarnished dignity. Like Timon of Athens I was (only slightly less misanthropic).

But there was always Mother. Mother was rich. Perhaps Mother could spare an allowance for her only child. I removed my cellular from my pocket and dialed, though I knew I shouldn't have. An artist does not beg. An artist does not cry for help, even when help is needed. An artist might take a bad job for the money now and again (see Mr. Brando in *The Island of Dr. Moreau*, for instance), but an artist never expects money without work.

…But no one's perfect, damn it. I was *hungry*, all right?

"Joel? Is that you, dear?"

"Yes Mother, it's your only son. I have bad news. Terrible news. The worst news imaginable. I've been jettisoned from the theater company. Someone else's fault, not mine."

Silence on the other end. Then, "Well that's fortunate. Now you can finally do what your father wanted and get a real job."

"It isn't *fortunate!*" I screeched. "It's the opposite of fortunate. My real job *is* an artist. A *thespian*. Not some work-a-day dog born on Wall Street."

"You were born in a hospital, dear."

"Whatever. The point is, Mother, I need money. Ten thousand dollars at a bare minimum."

Another pause, followed by a sigh. "Not this time, dear."

By the muses, the very world was against me! I wasn't asking for much—only enough to keep myself alive (and perhaps a bit extra for some decent head shots). But even that was taken from me!

"I can't help you with this acting nonsense any longer, dear," said Mother, "and I've an appointment to play tennis with the neighbors at 12. You'll just need to—"

The line went silent. I looked at the screen and found a

brief but disheartening message: SERVICE NO LONGER PROVIDED.

Alas, I'd forgotten to pay the cellular bill.

I wept for a time. After weeping, I wandered. After wandering most of the day, I happened upon a street performer at an intersection, one of those near-homeless creatures that stand motionless all day for money.

I stopped and studied the man. With all the silver paint layered upon his face, he might've passed as an android. I dared not draw too near, but I did take a single step closer.

"What is your name, sir?"

The human statue said nothing.

"Ah. A dedicated performer. I can admire that— though the rest of your act is rather bland, if I may be so bold. You no doubt think yourself an actor, but really, *anyone* could do that."

I chuckled to myself, then stopped. A dark thought had entered my mind.

"Were you a true thespian once, my good man? Tell me you weren't! Tell me you've always practiced this inferior art form, and that you weren't forced into it after being ousted from every other medium of performance. Tell me that."

The human statue said nothing, though I fancied I saw a bulging vein forming on his forehead.

"I'm afraid," I confessed. "I'm so *afraid*. This world is changing around me, and it doesn't even know I exist. I'm afraid I might turn into *you*, a man without screen or stage, a man banished to the streets." I sniffled. "Here. You look like you need this."

I checked my wallet for a dollar to place in his upturned cap, then found only a single twenty dollar mark and decided against it. As I walked away, I swear I heard a voice mutter, "Asshole."

I resumed my walk to nowhere. What else was there to do? I had no life anymore, I had no hope, and…

A voice said: "It just doesn't work like it used to, Godfather. What can I do?"

A second voice said: "You can act like a man!"

I turned slowly. I knew that voice—the second, not the first. I would know it anywhere. Yet it was wrong, somehow, like hearing a Bach symphony played by a third-rate fifth-grade band. It was the voice I knew, but also, somehow, *not*. I turned, and looked, and screamed.

There, upon a three-dimensional hologram device in a shop window, was Mr. Marlon Brando. But it was not Mr. Brando, not truly. The face was the same; the cheeks puffed out, the eyes slightly crinkled, the chin drooping, gray streaks through slicked-back hair. It wore a tuxedo with a black bow tie and a red flower, just like the real man had done so long ago. The image looked so damn *lifelike*.

But Marlon Brando had never done such a thing as this.

This simulacrum of Mr. Brando passed a blue cardboard box to a scrawny, nervous-looking fellow on the other side of a desk.

"I'm gonna give you an erectile dysfunction tablet you can't refuse," said the false Brando. The scrawny man looked at the box and smiled, and then the commercial cut to the product name: Hardzyte. The tagline: "Grow Great!"

I closed my eyes. I closed them because I could not look at the world. They'd done it. Hadn't Garth Sharpe said that they would?

Hell, we could even recreate Marilyn Monroe if we wanted to.

But they hadn't done it to Marilyn Monroe. They'd done much worse.

I turned and slumped against the glass window. I wept.

I can't say how long I was there, but eventually, someone poked his head from the door—the shopkeep, it seemed.

"Hey. Buddy. You mind cryin' somewhere else?"

I don't recall what he said next. I don't think I ever heard it. I found myself marching across the street, even as cars honked and sped within inches of me. A sporting goods store lay ahead. I stepped inside, used the last of my funds on my purchase, and stepped back out into the street. I held my new prop close, caressing the smooth ash wood, smiling at the words "Louisville" and "Slugger."

The bell chimed happily when I stepped into the hologram store. The shopkeep stood behind the counter, reading intently on his mobile phone. He looked up as I entered.

"Hey. I thought I told you to get outta here."

I said nothing. I instead turned my gaze to one of the projection apparatuses, a cluster of fan blades whirring and somehow forming a three-dimensional image. It currently ran an advertisement for a celebrity rehab program.

"This is for *art*," I murmured, and took the bat to the device.

Plastic showered down like little snowflakes. *Merry Christmas, Joel,* I thought to myself. *Entertainment, that torturous demon-deity that you love/hate so much—you've finally defeated it!*

I cradled my weapon. There was total silence in the store now—but my work was not yet finished. Another hologram generator waited beside me, and another beside that, and another, and another, and another. A whole army of them.

I brought the bat down upon the terrible things. More monsters slain. Smash, smash, smash!

I wound up for another swing, idly wondering why I'd never tried out for my high school baseball team, when a hand gripped my arm. Who could it be? I turned and found the shopkeep, the miserable oaf who'd mistaken me (*me!*) for a common bum.

"You goddamn maniac! You're destroying my shop!"

I wrenched away and managed another few hacks. But soon thereafter, the shopkeep and several misguided patrons wrestled me to the ground and subdued me. I might've shouted a few things I shouldn't have, might've bitten a finger or two, might've spat in someone's eye. As they love to say on those police procedurals, it all happened so fast.

In hindsight, I'll admit I might've overreacted. Just a bit.

ACT III: WHEREIN OUR HERO IS REDEEMED

The rest of that ordeal is lost to me. I remember sirens and cold shackles, flashing lights and a long car ride, then a cell with steel bars. I'm sure I spent an eternity in that place. I begged for food, water. They refused to give me anything, even though I was dying, dying slowly.

(I found out later that it had been three hours in total —but it really did feel like an eternity.)

In a fortuitous bit of deus ex machina, Mother took pity on me and swooped in with her cadre of lawyers. They managed to keep me out of prison. No one was hurt, after all, though the prosecutors claimed someone could've been. I deny it. An overreaction it might have been, but it was a controlled overreaction. Anyone who watches the security footage can see it plainly. Why, with a bit of rehearsal and some decent direction, I daresay I could've purged the store's entire inventory.

Still, the court appointed me a therapist to work on my supposed anger problems. We meet every Tuesday at seven. Her name is Dr. Wanda and I'm quite fond of the candy jar she keeps in her office.

Otherwise, I spent my days in bed at Mother's estate. She had suddenly become much more chipper, no doubt thinking my acting career was finally dead. I forbade her from turning on a single hologram in the house, for fear that I might see that revolting commercial again.

I must confess…I'd never been so low in all my life. For hadn't the scene in the television store been the perfect metaphor for computer-generated actors themselves? They could not be defeated, I realized. No matter how many devices I smashed, no matter how many baseball bats I bore, there would always be another hologram on another stage and another image on another screen. Like the hydra of the Ancient Greeks: for each head removed, two others took its place.

Mother entered the room with a telephone. "Someone to speak with you, dear."

"No Mother, please. Please leave me here to die. To die with my career."

"Don't be melodramatic, dear. He's being very patient and he sounds very important."

I frowned at Mother, but took the phone nonetheless. "Joel Henry Desmond speaking."

"Yeah. This is Barry French."

I waited for an explanation of who the hell Barry French was, but it seemed none was forthcoming. "Who the hell are you?"

"Ha," said the voice on the other end. "Funny. Hey, you have an agent? I should probably be talking to your agent, but I can't find him. You know you're hot shit right now."

"My agent's dead to me, and—wait…I am?"

"Sure. Your little tirade got on video. Some shopper filmed it and put it on the net. Went 'viral,' as the kids call it. Obviously you don't know much about this kind of thing. I do. I've been in TV for 30 years, and I know a guy I want when I see him."

"But…but I'm not a computer image. That's all anyone wants."

"For movies and series TV, sure. But I'm talking about reality TV, Jake."

"It's Joel."

"Like I said…reality TV. It's alive and well. I need real people, real emotions, real anger management issues. Like yours. I want you on my show."

We spoke at length. Mr. French informed me I would be appearing on the 16th season of a reality dating show entitled "RoboDate," in which I and nine other men would be paired up with ten women, five of whom were cyborgs. The allure of the show was to see who would fall for the cyborgs and who would discover "the real broads," as Mr. French so eloquently put it.

"You'll be on with an NFL wide receiver, a former kid actor, and that senator who got busted for boinking teenagers in Seven Eleven bathrooms. Real bunch of winners, kid. You'll fit right in. Whadya say?"

RoboDate. Perhaps it was beneath me. Perhaps I should not have degraded myself by even considering an appearance on it. Perhaps I'd regret this decision for the rest of my life.

Perhaps…

I gave him my answer.

I hung up the phone and called politely to Mother, asking for a television set, a vintage one, post haste. When she brought it, I stood from my bed, stooped low, and I kissed that television set, right on the screen.

Thus entered the revival of my acting career, stage right, and with a flourish.

VIRUS / AFFLICTION / CONDITION / CURSE

I: A FOREWORD

This letter I hold is from my mother. It's our first contact in almost a year.

I know it's from her before I open it, despite the lack of a return address. Maybe it's the pristine cursive handwriting or the generic bird stamp in the upper right-hand corner. Maybe it's the simple oddness of someone sending me a letter and not an email. Or maybe it's just intuition. Whatever it is, I know it's from her.

Upon tearing the seal, I find that same flowing script covering a sheet of lineless cream stationary. I read it. And again.

I've always been more like my mother than I meant to be. I suppose this letter confirms it.

II: SEVERAL INTERVIEWS (AND A TRANSCRIPT)

Mandy Stackhouse guzzles a 24-ounce can of SinApse and grimaces, then slams it on her desk, adding to a growing collection. Her eyes are red-rimmed and she has a sleeping bag laid on the floor of her office.

"You want any sushi? Fucking *supreme* sushi a block over, and they deliver."

I tell her no thanks and silently marvel at this woman's lifestyle. She will later reveal that she hasn't been home in the past week. She's had fresh clothes delivered to her by her girlfriend, who lives a few blocks beyond the fucking supreme sushi place. Mandy has snuck in the occasional late night shower at the gym across the street, to which she is not a member but somehow gets into, anyway. Her diet has consisted of delivery food, SinApse energy drinks, and Cheez-Its for the duration.

"Big trial," she explains. She's not wrong. Mandy Stackhouse is the defending attorney for Dalton Thomas. Turn on your TV and you'll see something about him.

Thomas is where he is because he killed his neighbor on the night of Jan. 8. He doesn't contest that fact—it's the state's capital murder charge he (and Mandy) are fighting. In fact, they're pleading not guilty by way of a defense entirely new to the American legal system: When Thomas killed his neighbor, he was not a human, and therefore not capable of stopping himself. He was a werewolf.

"Is a plea deal on the table?" I ask. Mandy evades the question. She's good at that.

"My client turned himself in three times. Three times he went to the local police station and warned them about what might happen. We have the tapes from the lobby. Six different officers spoke to him, and not a one did jack shit. Want another argument? I've got fucking millions. My client suffers from an affliction for which there is no cure—at least not until Randolph Tull and his people find one. My client did everything he could to protect others from his affliction: He locked himself in his house, notified family members of his whereabouts, tried the aforementioned meeting with local authorities. He did all he could, yet no one helped him. So riddle me this. What if your neighbor catches your cold? And his immune system is shit, so he dies from it. Are you now guilty of murder in the first degree?"

I consider that. "No. But I think this situation is different."

"I don't. My client doesn't. And we intend to prove it in court."

I shrug. "I suppose I have nothing further." Fortunately, I'm not a member of the jury.

"Anyway…" Mandy thumps her shoeless feet onto her desk. "The Supreme Court is doing us no favors, what with its collective head up its collective ass on the issue. Years of this virus in this country and they've done fuck-all."

Mandy then cites a Colorado case in which a woman changed into a werewolf while walking her daughter home from school. A passerby with a handgun and a concealed carry permit took it upon himself to shoot and kill the woman, right in front of her kid. The kicker of the whole thing: Nobody tried the guy.

"Like I said. The law doesn't give a shit about these people. And we're going to do something about that."

"You never answered my question. Would you and your client ever consider a plea deal?"

Mandy's eyes are alight. She usually exudes an air of congeniality—but not now. Now, I can tell she's pissed.

"Oh fuck no. We're fighting this thing to the dirty end."

We sit there staring at one another, trapped in the moment.

Knock knock.

"Sushi's here."

RANDOLPH TULL IS a hard man to reach.

You might recognize the name. Tull is the founder of Magniwest, a company which produces the parts that compose most commercial cell phones. As you might guess, it's a lucrative industry. Randolph Tull was named one of *Forbes* Magazine's 50 Richest People in the World just a few years ago. More recently, he's put his fortune to a singular use: funding research into the cure and prevention of *canis mutatio*, colloquially known as werewolfism.

There must be numerous unopened emails bearing my name which now rot in his secretary's inbox, yet I still haven't heard from him. I suppose the man has no time for interviews.

Nevertheless, I've continued to pester him on the off chance that he or one of his people notice. His money fuels Dr. Margaret Vine's groundbreaking werewolfism research, along with that of many others. He funded a series of cure for werewolfism ads, which were themselves a response to SinApse's ill-received though ostensibly pro-werewolf "Unleash Your Inner Wolf" ad campaign. He's offered no comment on either project. Perhaps this line from a recent article in *The New York Times* summarizes him best: "Randolph Tull's money talks while the man himself remains silent."

Still, by peering into Mr. Tull's past, one might infer why his money talks the way it does. According to my research, Tull's own father, Oliver, was a person with werewolfism. Three years ago, Oliver Tull was shot dead by a man named Clint Mason after attacking a neighbor while in the form of a wolf. This case bears an eerie resemblance to the Dalton Thomas case, right down to the victim living next door.

In the aftermath of the event, a source close to Randolph Tull claimed that Tull thought the shooting of his father was justified. According to the source, Tull said, "They did what they needed to do. My father wasn't my father anymore."

"SOME PEOPLE CALL IT A CURSE." Dalton Thomas shakes his head. "It's not. It's the best thing that ever happened to me."

When I ask him why, he takes no time to consider the question; it seems he already knows the answer. "Look at me. I'm the size of a high school freshman and I'm 26. I've been mugged four times in my life. Seriously, *four times.* Like I've got a 'kick me' sign taped to my back. But now no one bothers me. I just wear a short-sleeved shirt and people see the marks and they know what it means. Nobody comes after me anymore."

Thomas is indeed a small man. He's nearing five foot five if you round up, and he tells me he weighs just over a hundred pounds. He whispers as though a baby sleeps in the next room—only there's no baby. There's a man named Kremples who mutters about explosives while he sleeps. By the way, we're in Dalton Thomas's prison cell.

After a moment's pause, I say, "Describe the initial event for me. What happened?" (Note: I'm careful to use the word "event" instead of, say, "attack." There's growing resistance to the latter; it implies a violence that isn't always present.)

"Event?" He laughs. "Call it a kiss. I was hiking with

my dad and we heard whimpering, like a dog. I stepped off the trail and I found her under a tree, in the shade. I think some hunters must've shot her. She was dying." Thomas mumbles as if recounting a dream. "I bent down to see if I could help. Plus I was just curious. Have you ever seen one up close?"

"Never."

"They aren't what people think. She wasn't vicious. I think she wanted someone there when she passed. So I touched her fur, and it was soft, like fleece. You wouldn't expect that. I pet her. And when I did, she bit my arm." Thomas peels back a sleeve, revealing a short line of reddish indents. They're so faint they might be birthmarks. "Pinpricks. She wasn't trying to hurt me. It was like a survival instinct, you know? Just wanted to pass along the gift."

"Tell me about your trial. How do you think it's going?"

Thomas spreads his hands. "I've counted 13 witnesses so far—a scientist, a guy from an advocacy group for people like me, even Mrs. Finch. The prosecution asks them questions, Miss Stackhouse asks them questions, they step down, same with the next person. I don't pay too much attention to them, anyway. I just look at the jury and try to read their minds." He laughs though it sounds more like a sigh. "Hasn't worked yet."

"And the night of January 8. Can you tell me about that?"

Thomas's eyes cast downward at the mention of the date. "My mom always says gifts aren't free. So I guess mine wasn't either. I tried to protect people. Miss Stackhouse says I did everything I could. Maybe if the police had done something, maybe if there were laws in place to protect people like Mr. Finch from people like me, then maybe none of this would've happened."

"I see." A brief pause, during which I consider how best to phrase my next question. "Dalton. If Randolph Tull ever perfects the cure he's been working on. What would you do?"

He stares back with round, unblinking eyes. "Before the bite, what was I? Don't answer that—I'll tell you. Nothing. I was nothing, I was nobody. But now I know who I am. I'm a werewolf." Despite everything, he grins. "That's me now. That's Dalton Thomas. Why would I go back to being nothing?"

"To CALL it a curse is to make it sound supernatural. It isn't. It's actually quite scientific."

Roughly one month ago, Dr. Margaret Vine testified for the prosecution in the case of Dalton Thomas. Despite being 72, Dr. Vine still performs advanced medical research (most of which is funded by Randolph Tull). She works a full-time job, attends international conferences, and guest lectures at Johns Hopkins when she feels inclined. She even babysits her infant granddaughters every Sunday. When I asked for her secret, she answered, "Brussels sprouts." I can't tell if that was a joke or not.

Dr. Vine shows me a computer screen displaying two strands of DNA, side by side. She points to the one on the left. "A normal strand of deoxyribonucleic acid. Genetic building blocks. I'm sure you'll recognize the double helix from high school biology." Next, she jabs at the strand on the right. "Here we see the presence of *canis mutatio*. The difference should be obvious."

It is. The strand on the left has a double helix, as Dr. Vine stated. The one on the right, however, bears a third string of matter intertwined with the others. Where the first two are bluish and composed of small dots—representing something important, I'm sure—the third strand is fatter, with wider dots. It's also a lighter shade of the same blue.

(Note: Please forgive the upcoming chunky paragraph. Margaret Vine speaks in chunky paragraphs.)

"As I said, 'curse' is a misleading term for what we're seeing. What's worse, it's *inaccurate.* Equally so are the various PC labels offered by their Preservation Society, or whatever they call it." (An audible snort here.) "What we're looking at is a viral infection. The virus inserts itself into otherwise healthy cells, usually via bite and subsequent injection through the teeth, similar to the way a snake injects venom. There are other delivery methods: bodily secretion, aerosol transmission through sneezing or coughing, possibly even hereditarily, in rare instances. And yes, old-fashioned sex sometimes works, too. Whatever the case, the infected cells replicate the viral DNA, and..." She waves a hand at the strand on the right. "Observe the result. When compared with *canis mutatio,* the normal human genome is a Sunday morning crossword puzzle. Once infected, a victim's entire genetic code is rewritten. It's as though another organism now lives within and alongside the host. And if you inspect this other organism at a molecular level, you'll find a startling fact." She finishes the thought before I can ask. "It bears a distinct genetic similarity to *canis lupus.* The wolf."

I nod. "Hence the term 'werewolf.'"

"Precisely. Now I said this in court and I'll say it again now. How can something that so profoundly alters human genetics be considered harmless?"

———

CLINT MASON SHOWS me a picture on his phone, grinning while he does it. It's an image of himself standing over a mass of dark fur and muscle, rifle resting on his shoulder, eyes hidden behind blue-tinted sunglasses. His blindingly white smile is encircled by a coarse red beard, which possibly hasn't been shaven, ever.

"Biggest one I ever got." His smile somehow grows wider. "Not like it is in the movies, by the way. They stay hairy, even after you shoot 'em. Don't need to use silver, either—any ol' bullet works, provided you place it right. And the moon's got nothin' to do with the transformations —they're more or less random.

"Anyway, way I see it, I'm keepin the country safe from these things. Somebody's got to, cause the cops won't. They try and subdue the bastards. *Subdue* 'em." His laugh is not dissimilar to a revving chainsaw. "You imagine subduin' a three hundred pound animal? Like when a bear gets outta the zoo. You can fuck around with it, you can try herdin' it back into its cage, you can play nice. Or, you can go get a big fuckin' gun. God bless."

"But there's a person inside. Isn't there?" I find it necessary to press him here.

Mason shrugs. "Used to be. Once they get bit though, they're gone. Which is sad, really. The curse turns people into somethin' they're not, like a dog with rabies. But at the same time, you gotta think, how many people will this thing kill if somebody doesn't kill it first? I saw one squish a man's head like it was a grape. True story, I shit you not."

Clint Mason's name might sound familiar. That's because he's the same Clint Mason who shot and killed Oliver Tull, father of Randolph Tull, owner of Magniwest. The slaying launched him to fame and he's since become an internet vigilante sensation, a modern day Dark Knight sans the no-kill code. As of the writing of this article, his Instagram account has over 5 million followers.

Mason's eyes drift over my shoulder. I follow his gaze down the hall to another room where the door stands ajar.

There's a young girl within, maybe eight or nine years old, playing a game on an iPad. Mason introduces her as his daughter, Rachel.

I've noticed that Clint Mason tends to smile a lot. But when he introduced me to his daughter, that was when he smiled widest.

"I work at home during the day so I can be with her," he later explains over lunch. "She needs somebody around all the time. Some bad epilepsy." He pauses, then says this next part very seriously. "Imagine what one of them could do to my daughter if it got the chance. Remember what I said about them bitin' heads like grapes?"

"Have you encountered any legal resistance to what you're doing?"

"One time they brought me down to the station. Not like they could do anything. Laws protect people. They don't protect werewolves." Mason finishes his sandwich and tosses the plate into the sink.

"People seem to think the Dalton Thomas case might change all that. They're hoping the verdict might bring further clarity on the whole issue. What do you think?"

"Not much." He tips his chair back and stares out the window. "Far as I'm concerned, what I'm doin' is just peachy. Not homicide if you're not killing a person."

Clint Mason pops a green grape into his mouth and chews. I wonder if he realizes the irony.

<hr />

ONE INVARIABLY FEELS like an asshole when interviewing a grieving person. Yet that doesn't stop me from knocking on Sharon Finch's door. The sun has just begun its climb for the day; it casts golden-blue light upon everything, including a sign on the front door that reads, "Welcome Home."

I stare at that sign until it's pulled away by the swinging door. A woman wearing a dri-fit shirt stands in the space where the sign was. Her eyes flick over me.

"You must be a journalist," she says. Like she can smell it on me.

I introduce myself and confirm what she's already intuited.

"Now's not a great time." She stretches one calf muscle, then the other.

"You're going for a run."

"That's some sharp reporting right there."

I pause. For a moment, distant cars are the only sound between us. "I suppose I could join you."

Sharon Finch glares at me. She glares at my pea coat, my jeans, and my Converse. "Why? So you can write a sob story about how Dalton Thomas is misunderstood? About why we need to be nice to the werewolves?"

"It's not that kind of story. I'm just trying to understand this whole thing. As much as anyone can."

A long pause. Then she shoulders past me. "Don't fall behind."

I've had some odd interviews before. I once interviewed a musician in the middle of her concert. Another time I interviewed a patient hours after open heart surgery. But running alongside an interviewee—it's a first.

We set off down the street at a pace I know I'll struggle to maintain. Sharon Finch is clearly a runner and I am clearly not. At one time in my life I had interests other than my job. Not so much anymore.

"Just want to say I'm…sorry for your loss." (Note: The ellipses here and later represent me sucking in air.)

"Great," she says.

"Can you tell me a bit about…your husband?"

"I used to think Walt was invincible." (Sharon does not need ellipses.) "He was a vet. Gulf War. Came back here and became a security guard for a bank. Thwarted two attempted robberies. We used to run five miles together every morning." She casts a sidelong glance in my direction. I see no sadness in her eyes. More than anything, I see anger.

"How well…did you know…Dalton Thomas?"

Finch barely looks for oncoming cars before dashing across the street. "You end up knowing your neighbors, even when you don't want to."

"And his…condition?"

"His *condition.*" She gathers spit deep in her throat and splatters the sidewalk. "He's a werewolf. Not exactly a secret. Walt complained to the HOA but they didn't do anything."

"Can you tell me…about the night of…January 8th?"

"I was at work. Walt was getting our daughter from lacrosse practice. He went to grab the mail on his way out. That's when it happened."

"I'm sorry. I can't imagine…what it must be like."

"Then you're lucky." She stops, checks her time on her Fitbit. "The truly fucked up thing is, Dalton and his bitch lawyer claim he was protecting people from himself. But if that's true, why did he live near anybody? Why did he live in a goddamn cul-de-sac?" The muscles in her jaw flex. "Don't think I don't miss my husband just because I'm not crying."

"I'm so sorry for your loss, Mrs. Finch."

"Thanks. Means a lot. You know what I'm sorry for? I'm sorry nobody killed Dalton before he killed Walt. There's a quote for your article."

Sharon Finch turns and races down the sidewalk. She does not turn back, and I do not follow her.

"My name is Norris. I volunteer with the Lycanthrope Preservation Society." He pauses, clears his throat. "Is that, um. Is that a good intro?"

Norris Watts and I sit together on a park bench. We've known each other for maybe 10 minutes, yet we're somehow already on a first-name basis. That's fine with me, I suppose, albeit a bit surprising. Norris seems like the kind of guy who doesn't trust others much: He eyes passing strangers far longer than might be reasonably considered people watching. At any rate, he trusts me enough to do this interview.

"There's a common misconception about lycanthropes," he explains. "We prefer that term to werewolf, by the way. There's this, this um...*folkloric* image of them, I guess you'd say, like they're ravenous hunters who bite to kill. But based on our findings, this is rarely the case. When they're in their furry form, lycanthropes become territorial, kind of like wolves. If you set foot on their turf, they treat it as an act of aggression and it, well, it pisses them off. But when they bite, they're almost never biting to kill—it's almost always meant as a warning, or sometimes for reproductive purposes. When the bitten dies from a bite, more often than not it's an accident."

"Reproductive purposes. Can you expound on that?"

Norris shrugs. "We've all seen the Lon Chaney movies." (I don't know what kind of crowd Norris hangs with, but that statement doesn't really ring true. Anyway.) "The lycanthrope bites you, you become the lycanthrope. It's how they reproduce. Which is wild if you think about it. No other species on the planet does that. Sure, sometimes the genes pass from one lycanthrope to its kids, but that's hardly the primary method. Instead, they build on an existing foundation."

Norris reminds me, somehow, of a professor I had in

grad school. "What do you do to defend werewolves? Sorry. Lycanthropes."

"We've organized national and global protests against lycanthrope mistreatment. We've got branches across the country and in some parts of Asia and Europe. We do interviews like this to spread awareness. My kids even started a club at school. The more everyone learns about lycanthropes, the less they'll be feared."

"What are your thoughts on finding a cure? Stuff like what Randolph Tull is doing."

"A cure. Ha. Lycanthropes are so unique, and there are all these people who just want to erase them. It's disgusting. They're genetically different, sure, okay. But they're still people."

"I've spoken to some who think otherwise."

Norris's hands curl into fists. "If they really think that, then maybe they're the ones who've lost their humanity. Maybe the world would be better off without them."

He seems to realize what he just said, so he smiles apologetically. Yet he does not apologize for saying it.

HERE I'D LIKE to provide a transcript of a commercial from the "Unleash Your Inner Wolf" ad campaign launched by SinApse. Known for the popular energy drink (which you'll remember Mandy Stackhouse drinking), they've produced a series of advertisements based entirely around werewolves (or lycanthropes, if that's preferred). This commercial aired during this past year's Super Bowl:

FADE IN ON A SIGN. It reads "Werewolves Anonymous Support Group." In the background we see people filing into a room. Angle on folding chairs in middle of room. Ten or so people sitting in a circle.

Varying ages, ethnicities, and genders. The GROUP LEADER stands.

GROUP LEADER: I want to thank everyone for coming here today. I know this can be difficult but we hope it helps. Let's start with Doris. Doris, please tell us about your week.

DORIS is an elderly black woman wearing glasses and a dress. Beside her sits MIKE, a 20-something white man wearing a leather jacket. He holds a can of SinApse, label out, and drinks it every time the camera spots him.

DORIS: Well, last night I tore off all my clothes and went wandering in the woods.

MIKE: Been there, Doris.

GROUP LEADER: Thank you, Doris. Gabriella, do you have anything to add?

GABRIELLA is a young Hispanic woman in professional garb.

GABRIELLA: When I can't sleep, sometimes I go outside and howl at the moon. For like, hours.

MIKE: Oh, I totally get you, Gabriella.

· · ·

Group Leader: Thanks for your honesty. And how about you, Wesley?

WESLEY is an Asian man in his mid-30s wearing a hoodie.

Wesley: Last week I got mad at my dad, so I bit him.

Mike: Dude, Wesley. I bite people all the time.

Group Leader: Mike, is there something you'd like to say?

MIKE sips his SinApse.

Mike: Just partaking in the group chatter, my man.

Group Leader: Mike, I hate to ask. But are you even a werewolf?

Mike: Na brah. I just drink SinApse.

CUT to Mike with a background of cartoon stars flowing behind him. He holds a SinApse in one hand and tears open his shirt with the other, revealing thick chest hair. Quick zoom on fingers running through chest hair. Back to wide shot. Mike howls like a wolf.

· · ·

CUT to SinApse's yellow logo. In the background, we hear Mike screech.

MIKE: "UNLEASH YOUR INNER WOOOOOOLF!"

"YEAH, I worked on the werewolf Super Bowl commercial." Giovanni Fressi frowns for a moment, then says, "Why? You wanna complain about it?"

I find myself in his high-rise office early on this Saturday morning (Fressi works six days a week, purely by choice). He has an impressive view of the city from up here, of the tall spires of metal and glass nearby, the streets that ring them, and the tiny figures wandering below.

Fressi snaps the shades shut. "Sunlight," he explains. "Beams right in here. It'll cook ya. So who are you?"

I remind him who I am and what I'm doing here.

"Right. Okay. Well. I'm Giovanni Fressi, I'm SinApse's Senior VP of Advertising Experience. The werewolf thing was my idea."

"And how did it originate, exactly?"

"Well," Fressi sinks into his chair, making it squeal; he isn't a small man. "It occurred to me that nobody was really addressing this issue in the advertising world. Felt like an untapped opportunity. That tagline at the end, that 'unleash your inner wolf' thing. Turned out to be one of those love-it-or-hate-it lines, I guess."

My research has indicated mostly the latter. Though it was indeed one of the Super Bowl's most talked-about ads, many social media users questioned the intent behind the commercial. Most werewolf advocacy groups, including Norris Watts's Lycanthrope Preservation Society, downright condemned it. In an official statement on their website, they called it, "One of the most dull and insensitive advertisements regarding lycanthropes ever presented on television—or anywhere, for that matter." During her opening remarks in the Dalton Thomas case, Mandy Stackhouse even cited the commercial as a prime example of pop culture's misunderstanding of the werewolf community.

Yes, the commercial generated a lot of chatter. And even if little of it was positive, it seems people are talking about SinApse far more than they used to. Which likely means it was a success after all. Fressi knows this.

"We tried getting a celebrity endorsement for it. Somebody people would recognize, like a TV mom or whatever. When you're doing a topical ad like this, you want people to connect with the people you're doing the ad about. I called what's-his-name, Dalton Thomas, matter of fact, but he never got back to me." Fressi shrugs. "We couldn't get anyone else. Oh well."

I choose my next words carefully. "It seems there was criticism of the ad upon release. Care to comment on that?"

"Not really." It's getting difficult not to notice the basketball shot clock behind Fressi's desk, which has been steadily ticking down from eight minutes ever since I entered the office. "Millennials complained about the fact that we never saw the people as werewolves. They wanted to see a transformation or some shit like that. But the story of the commercial is about the people, not the wolves. We had a brainstorming team of 37 professionals on this project, and we all came to the same conclusion: show the people. People connect with people."

"Sure. But the wolf is part of who these people are now. So it's as if you're only showing half of them."

Fressi makes a fart sound with his lips. Behind him, our clock ticks lower. "Complainers complain. Whiners whine.

If it wasn't that, it would be the lighting, or the music, or the fact that we didn't have enough minorities sitting near the front of the wide shot. What was your opinion of it, Miss Williams?"

That's not my name. Evidently, Fressi's already forgotten it. I correct him, then say, "You don't want my opinion."

"Everyone at SinApse values any and all feedback."

"Okay. I think you took advantage of a sensitive subject. I think you exploited an entire group of people just to insert your brand into a conversation it shouldn't have ever been a part of. It's meant to align your company with righteousness and inclusion, when really you're just dumping lighter fluid on what's already a social and ethical garbage fire." I pause. "But that's just my opinion."

My speech turns out to be a buzzer beater; Fressi's shot clock screeches as soon as I'm finished. The sound is loud enough to make me jump, which pisses me off. Fressi doesn't jump. He switches off the buzzer, and when he turns back, he's smirking.

"What valuable feedback. Now get the hell outta my office."

TREVOR, whose name is not really Trevor, munches on the last of a soft shell taco. (For the sake of his privacy, I've changed his name.) He wears a white t-shirt and blue jeans, neither of which appear to have even a single stain upon them. Which surprises me, considering that he just came from recess.

"None of the other kids really talk to me." He sighs as though this is a regrettable but undeniable fact. "They think I'll eat them if I get mad."

Indeed, Trevor has an entire lunch table all to himself

today. I notice some kids across the cafeteria slumped against a wall, paper plates balanced on their laps. Nobody, not even the lunch monitors, seems willing to look in Trevor's direction.

"It's taco day. Do you like tacos?" He crunches into a hard shell this time, scattering shards over his plate.

I smile, I hope not too sadly. "Love them."

"Here." Trevor places a napkin in front of me, sets one of his two remaining tacos upon it. "I took too many, anyway. My mom says I shouldn't waste food."

I thank him. He seems like a nice kid.

I encountered a hell of a lot of resistance when searching for a child to interview. I wanted as many perspectives as possible. A kid's, for example, seemed like an important one.

The funny thing is, I did not find Trevor—Trevor found me. I had resigned myself to the inevitability that no kid would want to talk about something like this, until I got an email with this subject line: "Interview me! I'm a werewolf!"

In his email, Trevor told me he's been a werewolf since he was little. I later learned that he was in fact born with the condition; His mother has been a werewolf since she was young. As it turns out, Trevor is something of a scientific anomaly: He is evidence that werewolfism can be hereditary. Still, it's unclear exactly how the virus does or does not pass between generations.

There are a lot of questions I'd like to ask him. I'm not sure which ones I should go with. I've done hundreds of interviews—yet interviewing kids is still a challenge. "Trevor. Your mom told me you're seeking a cure for your werewolfism."

He dabs at his mouth. I've never known a third-grade boy to use a napkin properly, but there it is. He considers before answering.

"I was thinking about it the other day. I was thinking about like, if there were no werewolves, and that made me sad. Have you ever heard of Dodo birds? We learned about them in science class. They all died. I think it's sad that there's like a whole species that used to be around but now they aren't. And I guess they never will be again. So I don't know. I hope werewolves are still around someday. I just don't want to be one anymore. I just want to be normal."

―――――――――

III: AN AFTERWORD

I'm sure you're wondering what my mother wrote to me. I won't provide the exact content here. I'll just share the salient points.

About a month ago, my mother's doctor discovered an alarming chemical imbalance on her chart. They took further samples and sent them off to a specialist. The specialist got back to them, and they informed my mother of the findings.

As it turns out, my mother has werewolfism.

It's unclear how this happened. The doctors can't be certain of the origin date, but it seems the virus has been lying dormant in her body for three to four decades. My mother's best guess is that she got it from someone else without knowing it.

Though it's impossible to tell exactly when my mother contracted the virus, a slight chance remains that she had it when she had me. I'm 33 years old, which would fit the time frame the doctor suggested. Though rare, there have been some documented cases of werewolfism continuing through generations. As in the case of Trevor, for instance.

My mother urged me to get myself tested. I haven't.

I'm afraid of what I might learn. But my intuition, that same intuition that told me she'd sent me this letter, it's telling me now that I have werewolfism, too. Like I said, I've always been more like my mother than I meant to be.

By now I'm sure you've heard the verdict in the Dalton Thomas case—if you can call it that. After 20 hours of deliberation, an exhausted jury emerged. The forewoman explained to the judge that three jurors would not change their stance. Considering the amount of time they'd already spent deliberating, the forewoman insinuated that no decision could be reached.

The honorable Greta Yarwood disagreed. She sent the jury back into her courthouse's boiling deliberation room, where they continued to return almost every day for an entire month. (Lengthy as that may seem, it's not even close to the record for an American court. But it's still one hell of a long time.)

After 31 days, little had changed. In fact, according to the court transcript, the forewoman repeated the phrase "extraordinarily unlikely to ever come to a unanimous decision" four times.

Judge Yarwood reportedly took a long pause before speaking. Her official ruling reads as follows: "Though there is nothing I would like more, it appears we are unable to come to a unanimous decision. Based on the recommendations of the forewoman and the jury, I have no choice but to declare this case a mistrial, to be retried at a later date."

For those who never watched *Law & Order*, a mistrial is essentially a non-decision.

Of all the reports I did for this story, the third and the last linger longest in my mind. Dalton Thomas, who would never surrender his werewolfism, despite what he's been through. Trevor, who just wants to be normal. And then there's me, who can't decide which is right.

WINGS

"I can give you wings," he said.

That was all. That and an enigmatic smile, a smile that might've been warm or predatory or indifferent. All he wanted was an answer. A yes.

I gave it to him.

I returned the following Sunday. He invited me into his office and asked me to remove my shirt and lie down. He scratched Xs onto my shoulders with a felt-tipped marker. He set the wings next, cool and soft against my back.

"This might hurt," he said.

There were 14 silvery screws—seven for each shoulder. He hammered them first, pushed the sharp tips through skin, through flesh, into bone until the threads caught. Then he ground them downward, slowly. Each rotation brought the sound of cracking bones and trickling blood. He played Van Morrison while he did it.

I returned to him each morning, and each morning he offered me a smile and a hot chocolate with soggy marshmallows floating on the surface, and he asked, "May we continue?"

And, each morning, I nodded and said yes.

He forced the screws further. They held the wings in place, he explained patiently. He was always patient with me. I sobbed and I squealed, but I never asked him to stop. Afterward, only the wires remained.

"These connect to your nerves," he said, holding up blueish, rubber-coated tubes that resembled exposed veins. "The union will be difficult at first, I expect. But in a few months your body should accept them. The wings will be yours. And you'll fly."

I promised him I could be patient.

It took nine days to complete the procedure. I'd never felt such pain, never knew so much existed in the universe. I was a crossroads of agony. Every gash, every blow, every burn and bruise and break converged on my body. On my back.

But I would have wings. He promised me that.

Months passed. I inspected myself in the mirror each day. I stood naked, flexed the muscles in my shoulders, willed the wings to move, endured the pain. They did move. I'm sure they did.

I grew impatient. I called his office but no one answered. I drove there but he was gone. A custodian told me the police had taken him in the night. They said he was a criminal. They said he played cruel games with people's bodies. He wouldn't be coming back, the custodian assured me.

I did not fail to notice his eyes flick to the lumps on my back, beneath my coat.

———

IT'S BEEN a long time since then. Long enough. I've looked in the mirror each day and I know I've seen the wings move.

My wings.

I stand atop a building. A very tall building. My wings tremble in the wind. The pain is still there, always there, but I'm certain I won't feel it once I'm off the ground.

"I can give you wings," he'd said.

Someday, I'll find a way to repay him. For now, I step into open space.

THE MEGRIM

When the first child vanished in the night, I called on the High Temple for aid.

Piebald the Cobbler laughed at me for doing it. "You're always worrying, Pureman," he said the following day as we trudged over fresh snow. "Too much for a young man like you. These children, they go wandering, they come back. I've got a boy of my own, you know. Once this one starts missing his sweets and his bed, he'll return."

Yet a day passed without sign of the child.

Halfmoon was his name. He had a permanent smile and a skill for mimicry. His imitations of Asrith the Librarian, Glubb the Builder, Murple the Veteran, and myself always drew laughs. Our little town felt colder after his disappearance, and not only due to the constant snowfall.

Each day I awaited a response to my message from the High Temple. Though I sent my fastest bird as courier, there were many leagues between our village of Greengrove and, well, anywhere. What's more, we were surrounded by the Creaking Wood. Had my bird fallen prey to some creature of the forest? An owl? A hawk? Or something worse? Each day I waited. Each day I worried.

The second child disappeared three nights after the first. Her name was Zel and she was Bregna the Butcher's daughter. She used to cry when her mother cut meat because she pitied the dead animals. I inspected the ground outside her home for tracks, but the night's snowfall left nothing behind.

"I know who took them," Pia announced one afternoon while we prepared the Temple for evening prayers. She was my apprentice, a girl of 12 with a sharp mind and a sharper tongue. "Obviously, this is the work of a cannibal. Probably likes the meat from the young ones. It's more tender, I'd wager. Easier to mince."

I tipped my head to the sky. "My apologies for her morbidness, Goddess. She reads too many fictions."

"Not so many as you," Pia snorted. "When will you tell the Goddess I'm ready to be a Purewoman? You said I was the other day."

"I did. Though I believe I used the word 'soon.'"

"Soon. Maybe. Someday. Never. When adults say them, they all mean the same thing." She sighed. "Who do you suppose took the children, then?"

My gaze drifted out the window to the trees beyond. "I am not certain we're dealing with a 'who.'"

The snow fell, our village of Greengrove slept uneasily, and the next morning, my bird returned bearing a note. It was sealed with the mark of the High Pureman.

For Pureman Wendyll, it read on the outside. On the inside: *Help is on the way.*

A woman strode into Greengrove three days later. When she saw me, she spat.

I was certain she was a woman, yet she had the frame of a man: broad in the shoulders, thick in the arms, legs of solid rock. Her smile revealed several missing teeth. Her black hair was shaved on either side but lengthy down the middle; it formed a braid that hung to the small of her back and appeared heavy enough to double as a whip. She wore two axes, the heads of which peaked over either shoulder like stern metallic faces.

Again, she spat. I cannot say it was the best first impression.

The woman's next action, after the spitting, was to squint at me with a combination of curiosity and distaste. "Is this Greengrove?"

"It is," I replied. "Are you journeying to the capital?" I loved my town, but I had no illusions of its appeal to outsiders (or lack thereof).

"Been there before. It reeked. You the Pureman here?"

"I am. Wendyll is my name, Pureman Wendyll. And you are?"

The woman extended a hand. The hand was missing a pointer finger. That gave us something in common, for I too was missing fingers. Three, from my right hand.

"Name's Nairn Lockwood," she said. "Sent by your High Pureman to solve your little mystery."

Nairn Lockwood. *Nairn. Lockwood.*

I'd heard the name before—or rather read it. Nairn Lockwood was a mercenary from distant lands who'd fought battles and liberated prisoners and dared to accept missions no sane person would take. Nairn Lockwood was the subject of countless books ranging from fact to fiction to somewhere in between. Nairn Lockwood was called

Life-Ender, All-Warrior, Death-Blessed, and, for reasons I'd never discovered, No-Leftovers.

Nairn Lockwood was, in a word, legendary.

"Forgive me," I said, taking her hand and shaking it. "I had not expected…"

"What? A woman? And an ugly one at that?" Her laugh sounded like a boot scraped over gravel. "And I hadn't expected a schoolboy in a holy man's robes. How old are you, Pureman? Eleven?"

"One and twenty," I said, forcing a smile. "You misunderstand me. I had not expected the Temple to send someone of your reputation. Is it true you defeated the Champion of Luxdale in single combat?"

"Aye," she said, dipping into a pocket and retrieving a strip of dried meat. She chewed, swallowed. "Thrice. I killed him, then someone claimed his sword and called himself the new Champion of Luxdale, so I killed him too. Then a third one named himself Champion—killed that one next." She squinted at the sky. "Hmm. Was there a fourth one in there? Can't recall."

"And the conflict in the Nightlands. Did you truly negotiate the peace yourself?"

"More's the pity. That war was good fun. But Empress What's-Her-Name offered me thrice my weight in gold. And if you haven't noticed, I'm a hefty lass."

"And what of the Ventillion Mystery?"

"Wasn't much of a mystery," she mumbled through a mouthful of jerky. "Not after I solved it."

"And now you're here." I pursed my lips. "Which I'm happy for, truly happy, but…isn't this job a bit mundane for someone of your reputation?"

Lockwood said nothing. She only stared at me. The sound of wintry wind spoke for us.

"Lady Lockwood? Did you not hear me?"

"I did. But I don't answer stupid questions. Now…"

She finished the rest of her jerky in three titanic bites, then plunged her massive hands into her coat. "Shit on a brick, where's that damn writ? Supposed to get me free lodging. And more important, free food." (By now I was beginning to understand the "No-Leftovers" title.)

I inclined my head. "I'll take your word for it, Lady Lockwood."

"Oh no. No more of that 'Lady' shit. Lockwood is fine enough. Say that."

"Lockwood, then. We thank you for coming."

"Aye, whatever. Now where's the dead boy?"

I blinked. "Girl. The latest is a girl. There are three of them in total: First a boy named Halfmoon, then a girl named Zel. And a third one just last night. My...my apprentice. Pia." I swallowed down tears—I'd cried enough of those already. "They're not dead, Lady—I mean, Lockwood. They're only missing."

"If you say so. Show me where the last one disappeared."

"Her home? I think it best not to disturb the family at a time like this."

"Do they want the boy to be found?"

"Girl. She's a young girl."

"Whatever. Do they want her found?"

"Beyond a doubt."

"Then I'll do some disturbing. Lead on, Pureman."

Reluctantly, I led her through the streets (well, *street*) of Greengrove, to the home of Pia and her parents, Lara and Lorn. Our houses and shops were buried in snow, yet still I knew them: the leaning old library, Bregna's box-shaped butcher shop, Glendon Glubb's small abode, Mollo Murple's even smaller one. And, rising above them all, the looming bulk of Lendo the Versatile's mansion.

We reached the house a minute later. It was a modest dwelling, humble even for our little slice of the world. We stood on the edge of the village, mere yards from the trees of the Creaking Wood. Their bare branches reminded me of exposed bones. I dared not look too long.

"Here. This is Pia's home."

"'Is'? You speak of this girl as though she's still alive."

"I pray that she is, and the others. The Goddess shall protect the young and innocent. I'm sure of it."

Lockwood spat, then produced a blue sphere from another hidden pocket. "The Goddess protects nobody and nothing. In my experience, missing is usually dead. Cockatrice egg?"

I shook my head. Lockwood shrugged, then cracked the shell upon her knuckle and slurped the contents. "Mmm. I like them raw. Toughens the tummy." She tossed the remains aside, approached the house, and thumped the door.

I hurried after her. "Pia is a curious girl. Insatiable. No matter how much she knows about a subject she always wants to know more. She reminds me of myself in that way. One day she'll lead a Temple, and I'm sure she'll do a better job of it than I have. She's a kind child, a resourceful child, and she's only just gone missing. I do hope you'll be soft with her parents. This is a trying day for them. Will you promise me that?"

I stared at the mercenary. She stared back at me.

She said, "Sorry, did you say something? I wasn't listening to any of that."

The door swung open to reveal a woman and a man. The woman had thin lips and hair like straw. The man had a round belly and no hair at all. Both had red-rimmed eyes.

Lara and Lorn. Pia's parents.

"Pureman," said Lara, inclining her head. She then regarded Lockwood.

"This is our investigator," I explained. "Nairn Lockwood. She's come to help us find Pia."

"Greetings. You know the name. A pleasure to meet me, I'm sure. Yes, all the stories are true. By chance do you have any pickled basilisk tongues? I'm fresh out of snacks and still feeling a bit peckish."

Lara and Lorn gaped at Lockwood as though she was a speaking bear. "We...no. We have none."

Lockwood shrugged. "Show me the last place you saw her."

The couple led us through their house. It was a compact space, just a common area, two bedrooms, a hearth. The floorboards groaned with each step Lockwood took.

"Pia's room is here." Lorn pointed to a door, and then he began to weep. That made his wife weep, and together they excused themselves.

"Why do the bereaved always start crying before I can ask them questions?" Lockwood muttered.

I frowned at her. "Have you no compassion?"

"Com. Pash. Un." She shrugged. "Never heard of it." She pushed me aside and pressed into the room.

I am not a large man but Lockwood is a large woman. In that room there was barely enough space for us both. The window stood ajar, a detail which was common to all three disappearances. I relayed this information to Lockwood. "No noise in the night. No evidence of forced entry, not with any of them. Only open windows, like this."

Lockwood poked her head out the window. She looked left, right, up, down. She turned, leaned over the child's bed, and sniffed. "Are we to assume nothing's been touched since last night?"

"I believe so."

"Then look at the sheet. Tossed aside as if she rose from bed for a late-night pastry."

"What are you thinking?"

"I'm thinking about thinking. Hush." Her eyes bounced about the room: the bed, the door, each wall, back to the window. They stopped there. "A sleeper would have a clear view out that window, yes? Don't answer that —I'm thinking aloud."

She wasn't wrong. From her bed, Pia would see...

"...The Creaking Wood," I murmured.

"Aye. That." Lockwood poked at a gap in her teeth with her tongue. Then she sprang to the bed and dove under the sheets.

"Lockwood!" I cried. "What in the name of the Goddess are you doing?"

"Putting myself in the victim's shoes. Somewhat literally. Children don't wear shoes to bed, do they?"

"But—but you'll corrupt the scene."

"Or I'll have a sudden epiphany. Perhaps both. Now move, Pureman. You're blocking my view."

She was here to solve the mystery, I reminded myself. She was here to find Pia, and Zel, and Halfmoon. The High Pureman sent her to save our poor children. If she could do that, I could endure her rudeness. I released a breath, then stepped aside.

Lockwood stared out the window at the trees beyond. "I'm a little girl," she chirped. "Imagine I'm just an innocent girl dreaming of candy and sunshine and whatever the hell else the little shits dream of. I'm dreaming, dreaming, and then—ah! Who's that at my window? Pureman, stand outside the window for me."

"What? Whatever for?"

"For the sake of authenticity. I must needs visualize the event, and you seem the sort who lurks outside rooms at night. I'm asking nicely."

I don't believe she was, but I stepped through and hauled myself outside anyway. "Does this suffice?"

"It'll do." She took a moment to consider me. "Are you sure of your age, Pureman? You still look like a child to me."

"Now probably isn't the time for such talk, Lockwood."

"Very well, child. Knock on the window."

"Knock? Why must I knock?"

"Must you question my every order? Just do it!"

I knocked on the window.

"Not so loudly, you dolt. You'll wake the girl's parents and be found for the villain you are."

My face turned red. I do not often feel anger, but at that moment, it surged through me. "I did not commit this terrible deed!"

"Perhaps not, but you're acting. You know of actors, yes? You have one here in town, I hear? Actors pretend, and so must you. Softly, please."

I knocked. Softly. Lockwood nodded to herself. She rose, feigned drowsiness, then tottered to the window and climbed out, just barely squeezing through the frame. She stood there next to me and pondered. She stroked her chin with a finger—or would have, if the finger had been there.

"Sheets tossed aside, window unlatched, nothing broken, nothing heard. I do believe our girl went willingly to her captor."

A fine observation, yet one I'd already deduced with the previous two disappearances. I informed her of this, and she glared at me.

"Fine then. A step further. I believe we're looking for someone from your town, likely an older, charming presence. Someone others admire and respect. This is no stranger nor monster—this is someone the girl trusted, and trusted well enough to approach in the dead of night. What's the population of this place?"

"Forty nine," I said. "Or 50, if you count the babe in Lady Lobell's womb."

"That's our list. Next comes a process of elimination. I suppose we can start by scratching off the babe."

"But can you be certain we're dealing with a human?" I countered. "Could it not be something more...supernatural?"

"Supernatural?" Lockwood made a face like I'd just removed my clothes and rolled in the snow. "What's your evidence, Pureman? A sign from your Goddess?"

I pointed downward. Lockwood followed my gesture. Her eyes widened.

"Ah," she murmured. "Interesting."

Tracks. Tracks in the snow beneath our feet. Jagged, splayed shapes, monstrous and strange. Seven toes on the left foot, six on the right. Though our own tracks intermingled with them, these were significantly larger—perhaps two or three times the size. I had seen the tracks of the wyvern in a volume from the library, and the gray lurt, and the five-eyed lizapog. These tracks belonged to none of them. This was something much larger—and plainly not human.

I must admit, I relished the shock on Lockwood's face, however briefly. "We townsfolk already tried following them," I said. "They become lost among the underbrush of the forest. Yet their presence reinforces my theory. This was no human. This was the work of the Megrim."

"The Megrim?" She laughed. "But why not the Woolyman, or the Frostling, or the Naked Sprites of the Woods?"

I did not rise to her gibe. "Follow me," I said. "I have something you ought to see."

I said my goodbyes to Lara and Lorn, then hastened across town with Lockwood following. She did not hasten. When we finally reached my quarters, which adjoined the town's Temple, it was nearing midday. I turned the key and held open the door. "Boots off, please."

Lockwood entered, boots still on. I followed, barring the door on the cold behind us.

"You live in this mess?"

I suppose she was not incorrect in her assessment of my living quarters. Books and papers and notes and scraps covered every surface. With that space occupied, I'd taken to stacking books upon the floor to form towers, some of which reached eye level. An ink pot lay upturned over my desk in the far corner of the room. The ink had soaked into the surface, turning it shiny and black.

"It's a wonder you live here," she said. "It's a wonder *anyone* lives here."

"Thank you," I replied. "Are you an avid reader yourself?"

"Do I look like a reader to you?"

"No," I admitted. "Nonetheless, I believe this book might interest you, especially considering the circumstances of our present investigation." I offered her a tome, one which I'd reserved from Asrith's library a week prior. I'd read it before, long ago, as I'd read every book in our town's collection. Asrith made it her life's work to procure books from many lands and had succeeded marvelously. She owned stacks dating back to elder civilizations, foundational religions, even records of those who were here before us. All fascinating, all useful in their own way.

Lockwood frowned at the book. "Paper is best for wiping one's ass. Not reading."

"Excuse me?"

She repeated herself. Had she cloven my chest with one of her axes, the pain to my heart might've been less.

"But—but—but books are recorded knowledge. Books are chronicles of history and imagination. Books are distillations of human thought. Books are *magic*, Lockwood. How could you be disinterested in magic?"

She shrugged. "Books are the crutch of the inexperienced."

"How literary."

She snorted. "Tell me. Have you ever been outside this village?"

"Certainly. I've been along the Holy Road and some towns adjacent. And I've been to the High Temple itself."

"Anywhere else?"

"My place is with the people of Greengrove."

"Which means no." Lockwood pressed her tongue to the gap in her teeth. "Readers like you seem rarely to venture from your homes. Yet you claim knowledge of places you've never been to."

"Books are windows to distant lands."

"And a poor substitute for actually being there. Take this one, for example." She tapped the cover of the tome in my hands. "Why does it make you so sure these tracks mean anything?"

"I'll show you."

The spine of the book cracked as I opened it. It was a bulky leather-bound volume with a coat of dust which I could not seem to wipe clean. Every turn of the page sent a fresh cloud of particles into the air. It made me sneeze.

"Cover your mouth, you savage!" Lockwood barked. "I'll not be getting sick on account of you."

"Apologies." I flipped the book to my mark and passed it to Lockwood. "You'll want to read this section."

She peered down at the text. Her eyes flicked over it quickly. A bit *too* quickly. "Mmm. Yes. Right. Interesting."

I pursed my lips. "And what are your thoughts on it?"

"On what?"

"On what you just read. The section concerning the Megrim's nighttime slumber rituals."

Lockwood itched a scar across the bridge of her nose. "It's uh…it's fascinating."

"Lockwood. There are no nighttime slumber rituals listed there. The Megrim is nocturnal. That passage concerns the mating habits of the arctic puffin." I paused, wondering if there was a more tactful way to ask. None came to mind. "You can't read, can you?"

"Nonsense," she guffawed. "Of course I can. You think a hero such as Nairn Lockwood would be illiterate? Nonsense, Wendyll, nonsense."

That was the first time she called me by my name, I noticed. "Or truth. Read this for me." I pointed to the page on the right, the one truly about the Megrim.

She glared at me. "Fine, Pureman. I can't read. Not a word. Is that what you wanted to hear?"

"Yes. The Goddess appreciates an honest truth." It also explained how she hated books. No literate person can hate books. "Allow me." I cleared my throat and read aloud:

"'The Megrim is a monster born of woodlands and darkness. Its kind is reclusive and, for the most part, quite craven. It is a shambling, birdlike thing that walks on clumsy limbs but does not fly. It can be tracked by its toes, which number 13. The Megrim is detested and denounced by the Goddess Herself.'"

"Your Goddess again, eh? So these are religious texts."

"If that's what you want to call them."

"That's what they are. Aside from this book and those dubious tracks, what evidence have we that a Megrim even exists? Couldn't these texts be false?"

"Certainly not."

"Prove it, then." Lockwood unfurled her hands and spread them. "Prove your religion. Prove the existence of the Goddess, and therefore this Megrim. Go on."

I waited. I listened. Snow thumped as it slid from the roof outside. Wind whispered against the edges of my quarters. A crow cawed in the distance. "There. Do you hear that? There is your proof. Without the Goddess, none of this would be possible. Without her, nothing would exist."

"And I say it's all happenstance. I say this all exists because of a cosmic fart. Disprove that."

"Who did the farting, I ask?" Perhaps not the most eloquent theological argument, but there it was. Pureman Caladon certainly wouldn't approve, were he present. In his rhetorical essay *Words and Influence*, Caladon deemed it a weak logical appeal to answer a question with another question. (He did not, however, comment on the rhetorical value of discussions of flatulence.) Nevertheless, I pressed on. "Who set everything in motion? If nothing existed before anything existed, someone must've created it all. It had to be the Goddess."

"Or, more likely, it was something none of us will ever understand. Besides, we're getting off topic. I have a reason for being here. Well, several thousand of them, actually." She guffawed. Then, seeing my face, she looked away and coughed.

"How *dare* you."

"It was a joke, Pureman. Nothing more."

"That was no joke. I may be younger than you, mercenary, but I'm no fool. I catch your meaning. You're only here for the money."

She smiled suddenly, crossed her arms over her chest. "Fine then. Yes, I'm only here for the money. Half when I accepted this mission, half when I finish it, all adding up to a sizable sum. You do know what 'mercenary' means, yes? Perhaps you've read the definition in one of your books?"

"I'd only thought you might care for the lives of the missing children."

"Insofar as they're worth something to me."

"You're despicable."

"I'm hardworking. Now make your point or be done with it."

I did, albeit grudgingly. "This text goes on to describe the Megrim as a collector. It snatches small animals—or in our case, children—the way a magpie snatches jewels. It covets them but does not necessarily devour them. Therefore, I believe they may yet be alive. We need only find them."

"If you're so sure you have the answer, why call on your High Temple in the first place?"

"Because I'm no hunter." I nodded to the axes strapped across her shoulders. "And I don't have a pair of those."

That made the mercenary grin. "You're missing a pair alright. Fine, Pureman. You have your theory and I have mine. We'll see which is correct." She stood and opened the door, blasting the room with cold air. "Ladies first."

I shot up from my seat. "Lockwood, I really must protest. We should begin our search with the woods. That's where the Megrim must've taken them—"

She spun about, and for the first time since we'd met, I realized just how much taller she was than me.

"Which of us is the hired expert, Pureman?"

"Well, you are, but—"

"And which of us requested my expertise?"

"I suppose I did. But Lockwood—"

"That makes me the leader. And, as leader, I say we start with the most likely culprits: the townsfolk. Not some storybook monster."

"But what of the tracks?" I insisted. "How do you explain those?"

Lockwood stepped outside. "Tracks can be easily faked. Innocence, less so. Especially when I'm asking the questions. Now take me on a tour of your town, Pureman. I'd like to meet my suspects."

4

And so began the next phase of our quest. I cannot say my apprehension entirely dissipated, but Lockwood was right. She was the High Pureman's agent, and so the investigation was hers to direct. Besides, the sooner we exonerated my fellow townsfolk, the sooner we could search for the Megrim. The mere thought brought cold sweat to my back, despite the chill in the air.

Lockwood strutted down the road with her chest puffed out, powdery snow swirling around her boots like mist. She jabbed a meaty thumb toward a building on our right. "What is this thing?"

"That," I informed her, "is the pride of Greengrove. Our library."

The mercenary laughed. "I've seen ruins in better condition."

Indeed, the structure had deteriorated, even from its poor state in my childhood. Its walls bent inward, its roof slumped forward, and every passing breeze made it squeak and shudder. Smoke puffed from a chimney that leaned sideways.

"Books and covers, Lockwood, books and covers. You know you must not judge them so. Within our library lies one of the most vast and diverse collections of books this world has to offer. Stacks on the great Mythelian Empire.

Volumes of the philosopher Sho-Shenn's personal texts. The original drafts of Countess Krezemo-Hezemo's treatise on geriatric lovemaking."

"Now you're just making things up."

"I would never. It all lives in our library. Anything you could possibly want to learn on any subject."

"What joy! Perhaps I'll discover how to shut you up." And with that, she marched to the entryway.

As Lockwood reached for the door, it swung open. A man emerged, stepped forward, and bounced off her. The man sprawled. The stack of books he'd been carrying tumbled into the snow.

"Why Mr. Glubb," I laughed, pulling the poor man to his feet. "Are you alright?"

Glubb was a round fellow with a thinning pate and a bulbous nose. "Only confused. Has a snowdrift formed in the doorway while I was inside?"

"Not snow," said Lockwood, grinning. "Go on, Pureman. Tell him who I am."

"Glendon Glubb," I said, "meet Nairn Lockwood. She's here to find our missing children."

"And eat," Lockwood added.

Mr. Glubb gazed upon her the way I might gaze upon the Goddess incarnate. "I've read so much about you, my lady. You're a hero, you're *the* hero, you're...I..." He took a rattling breath. "Might I trouble you for an autograph?"

Lockwood suddenly seemed a deal more interested in the man. "Why certainly. And why only one? Why not more? Fetch paper and quill, good sir, I'll sign this very—"

"Perhaps another time." I smiled at Mr. Glubb and patted him on the arm. "Lockwood is busy searching. There's no time for signatures."

The mercenary glared at me, then shifted her attention back to Mr. Glubb. "As the holy boy said, I'm here to find your missing runts. Where were you last night?"

Glubb's face was always somewhat pink. Lockwood's question turned it scarlet. "Why, I was at home, reading. I wouldn't dare go out in this cold, not while the snow falls. It's unnatural, all this snow. Not natural at all."

"And what were you reading?"

"A book, just—"

"Name it."

"*The Boy, Four Mugs of Ale, and the Extract of Dragonsbane.* From the library. An adventure story."

"Pureman. Is that a real book?"

I blinked. "Of course. Though not an especially good one, I'll admit. Surely you do not think—"

"And you. Grub, or Glove, or whatever your name is. Can anyone confirm your story?"

"I live alone. But I read by firelight last night. My neighbors would've seen the glow at any hour. Ask them, ask them please. I would never lie to you, great hero."

"Hmm." Lockwood inspected her nails (which were dreadfully dirty, I might add). "Sounds like something a liar might say."

"But—but—"

I stooped and collected an armful of fallen books, brushing snow off as I went. "Here you are, Mr. Glubb. I apologize for the disturbance."

"That's quite alright, Pureman Wendyll. I thank you. Careful of the snows. There's something evil about them, I'm sure of it…" The man gave one last parting glance at Lockwood before hurrying away.

"You dismissed my suspect," she growled.

"Glendon Glubb has lived in this town longer than I've been alive. He's a good man, a simple builder. He would never hurt a child. Besides, I'm sure if we asked his neighbors they'd confirm his fire was indeed ablaze. He reads by firelight almost as much as I do, I'm told."

"Which would only prove that his fire was lit. Not that he was near it."

"So that's the way of it, then? You'll accuse everyone in town before even considering the Megrim?"

"I'll consider it when it's worthy of consideration. Now let's meet your librarian." She entered the library. I followed.

The familiar aroma of musty paper and old knowledge greeted us. As my eyes adjusted to the dim interior, I saw the books. So many books. More books than I had in my study, more books than I'd ever seen anywhere else. Labyrinthine shelves stuffed with them, floorboards stacked with them, even a few perched upon the door frame above us. And there, behind the counter and surrounded by columns of precariously piled volumes, stood Asrith.

As the stories went, Asrith had been the librarian in town even before there was a library. Like the building she spent her days within, she appeared to fall inward upon herself. Her neck drooped and her shoulders sagged, yet her candor was no less cutting than ever it had been.

"Good day, Asrith," I said. "We're here to—"

"Librarian," Lockwood barked. "I'm here to—"

"I can guess what you're here for." Asrith's brown eyes met mine, then Lockwood's. She did not blink. "This is the one the High Ass-man sent, eh? Don't bother denying it. Just ask your questions and be gone. And be quick about it. I have books to shelve."

"Very well." Lockwood leaned against the counter. "Where were you last night?"

"Here. Inventoried new donations until well past dark. Locked up after that."

"Fear not, Asrith." I tried to sound cheerful. "She must ask everyone."

Neither of them acknowledged me. Lockwood said, "And I take it you were alone?"

"Always am. Which makes you doubt my story, doesn't it?"

"Somewhat. Except that you're an old woman who's barely able to stand for more than five minutes. Look at you. You're shaking. You could hardly wrangle one child, let alone three. Why, you might drop dead at any moment."

Silence. I felt the sudden compulsion to apologize on Lockwood's behalf. I opened my mouth, ready to invoke the forgiveness of the Goddess herself, then stopped. Asrith was laughing.

"I like this one," she guffawed. "You're a nasty wench, now aren't you?"

More laughter, this time from Lockwood. "The nastiest, you old goblin. Now tell me. Did you see anything strange last night on your walk home? Anything out of the ordinary?"

"No. Thought I heard something up near the actor's place, but my ears play tricks on me these days."

"Ah yes, the actor. What's his name again?"

"Lendo the Versatile," I said. "A renowned performer, a member of the Everlasting Players. He returned from a tour of the east but a few weeks ago. He appreciates his solitude and so owns a winter home here in Greengrove."

"Actors are whores," Lockwood announced, in the way one might remark upon the weather. Then she turned to Asrith. "Good day to you, noble hag. Perhaps you'll reconsider your profession. Try something less boring with the years—or months—you have left."

Asrith roared with laughter. "Slim chance of that. But I appreciate your frankness, you rude beast. Luck to you. And *you*." She flicked her eyes on me. "Best not return overdue books again this month, young Pureman Wendyll."

I smiled nervously. "Certainly not, Lady Asrith. Good day." Lockwood and I stepped outside.

The sun was still up, though by now it had begun its descent. "I'm glad you did not accuse Asrith of taking those children."

"Oh, I wanted to. Decided against it."

"Great Goddess, Lockwood. She's just an old woman! She can't even lift a book over her head any longer. I myself stack the higher shelves for her these days."

Lockwood snorted. "I once pretended to be a corpse so I could sneak out of a prison. Doesn't mean I was truly dead. Pretending isn't all that difficult."

"Now listen here—"

"The librarian's a suspect, too. Now show me that actor she mentioned."

Lendo the Versatile's home was just up the main road, near the forest. It was the largest residence in Greengrove, though, in my opinion, also the least welcoming. Lendo had made addition after addition as his career blossomed and now the place resembled some sort of unchecked fungal growth.

"This house is…" Lockwood pursed her lips, "…messy."

"It is," I admitted. "But Lendo is a fine man, and a generous one. He's done much for this village in his time here. We value him both as a neighbor and as an artist."

"Generous?" The mercenary cocked an eyebrow. "By which you mean he's donated to your Temple. Is that it?"

"If you must know…yes. But no one can buy my friendship. Anyone who lives in Greengrove is a friend of mine."

"My friendship can be bought. In fact, that's usually how it's done. After you."

We climbed the house's spiral staircase to a second-floor entrance. The walk left me winded, and I wondered (not for the first time) if it might do me good to set aside my books and get outside more often. After we solved our mystery, perhaps. I knocked.

A man in velvet robes answered the door. He had both hands clasped behind his back and a cloth draped over one shoulder, along with a look of profound annoyance. Patches of blonde hair sprouted about his cheeks, no doubt meant to be a beard. "What is it?"

"Themus," I said, smiling. This was Lendo's manservant. He'd only been hired a few weeks ago, though I prided myself on knowing the names of everyone in town. "Greetings to you. Is the master of the house present?"

"He is," Themus clucked. "Alas, he is working."

"That's convenient," said Lockwood. "So are we." She sniffed the air once, twice, thrice. "Is that bacon I smell?"

"Hear me, strange woman. Master Lendo is rehearsing for an upcoming role. His rehearsal requires seclusion, discipline, and the utmost concentration. Master Lendo therefore cannot speak with either of you. Come by another day, perhaps he can assist you then."

"Worry not. We'll only be a moment." As if she was the wind and the manservant a leaf, Lockwood brushed Themus aside with a sweep of her arm and proceeded forward. I hastened to follow.

The interior of Lendo's home was furnished and decorated much like the castles of my favorite novels: exotic paintings, modern sculptures, bearskin rugs, crackling fires in the hearth of every room. I hurried to keep pace with the mercenary. Themus followed us.

"What do you think you're doing, Lockwood?" I hissed. "You cannot force your way into a person's home."

"Why not? I knocked. The door was open. And I smelled something delicious."

By then we'd arrived at the kitchen. Pots and pans hung from the walls, a wood-fire oven blazed in one corner, and indeed, the smell of bacon filled the room. A cook held several strips on a frying pan above a fire. (I cannot say I knew her name. A new arrival, perhaps?) She stared at Lockwood as the meat sizzled.

Lockwood approached the cook. "Do you mind if I...?" She reached into the skillet, bare-handed, and plucked a strip. She held it over her mouth and dropped it into her waiting jaws. "Marvelous," she said through bites, clapping the cook on the back. "Seared to perfection, my dear." She ate the remaining strips in rapid succession, seemingly oblivious to the heat.

The cook gaped at Lockwood.

The next moment, Themus stormed into the room. He'd finally caught up to us. "Now listen here, you brutish she-beast. You cannot barge into Master Lendo's home and eat Master Lendo's food without Master Lendo's permission."

"How rude of me. Let's find him and get his permission, shall we?"

"Wait," I said. "Lockwood—"

But she'd already vanished into another room. She seemed to be following a sound, something with a jolly tune. I followed her and Themus the manservant followed us both, screeching like a seagull.

We passed through a bedroom, beneath an archway, down a hallway lined with lewd erotic artwork. The music grew louder. Lockwood turned a corner and stopped.

We'd entered a vast room with a domed roof and a gleaming hardwood floor. A woman and a man awaited inside. The first I did not recognize: she was a young lady seated upon the floor with a harp in her lap. She'd been the one playing the music we'd heard. The sound was heavenly, though it came to an abrupt halt as we entered. The other person in the room, the man, laid upon the floor, one foot crossed over the other, fingers tracing circles through the air as though conducting a symphony. Lendo. His head flopped to the side. "Who the bloody blazes are you?"

"Depends on who you are." Lockwood strode forward, her boots thumping against the hardwood. "Are you Lumbo?"

The man sat bolt upright. He wore a luxurious bathrobe with, it appeared, nothing beneath. Based on the expression upon on his handsome face, you'd think someone had just booed him during his curtain call.

"*Lendo,*" he hissed. "Lendo the *Versatile*. First Thespian of the Everlasting Players." He glared at Themus as the manservant entered. "How did this rude intruder enter my home?"

"My profuse apologies, master," Themus wheezed, hands on his knees. "She forced past me."

Lockwood revealed an incomplete grin. "Nairn Lockwood. Let me know if you'd like an autograph."

I stepped between them. "Lendo, I apologize. Lockwood here is investigating our missing children, and in her zeal to find them I do believe she's overstepped the dictums of politeness."

"She most inducitably has," Lendo growled.

Inducitably? Did he mean indubitably? I ignored the mistake.

"I want you out of my home," Lendo continued. "This instant. I'll not tolerate interlopers while I'm working."

"Working, eh? Looked more like lounging to me."

Lendo's smooth face turned the color of his pouting lips. "How dare you, woman! That was the artistic process. Mine latest role requires fine music to untether human emotion from my mind."

"I don't know what that's supposed to mean and I suspect you don't, either. Now tell me...where were you last night? And be plain about it."

"Here. All night. Rehearsing for my next performance, as I'm doing now." He waved a hand at the harpist. "You wrong me with your questions. I resent your indication."

One mistake I could ignore. But two?

"Implication," I corrected. "I believe you mean implication."

Both Lendo and Lockwood glared at me, so I fell silent.

"I'm merely asking a question," Lockwood continued. "Who can corroborate your story?"

Themus the manservant stood forward and poked out his chin. "I can. Master Lendo speaks truly."

"Yes," the harpist agreed. "He was here all night. I'm sure of it."

Lockwood cocked an eyebrow at her. "Oh, I'm sure you're sure of it." The harpist blushed and looked away. Lockwood pressed on. "Your librarian claims to have heard a noise near your house last night. What might that have been?"

"How the Goddess should I know? An owl? A nightingale? Some other creature of the forest? The woods are nearby, as anyone with eyes can see."

The man's words reminded me of my own theory. "Lendo. There were tracks in the snow where young Pia was taken. Tracks of a grotesque and birdlike sort. I believe they belong to a monster called the Megrim. Have you seen any sign of such a creature?"

Lendo frowned. "The Megrim? Why, that's only a myth."

"A myth," Lockwood repeated. "You do know the meaning of the word, yes?"

Lendo scowled at her. "I will not be mocked and accused in my own home. Out, now, both of you. The High Temple will hear of this intrusion, Pureman Wendyll, I promise you. He'll be hearing an entire *soliloquy* about it."

I opened my mouth to say more, yet Lockwood hooked me about the shoulders and steered me toward the door.

"Worry not, Lugdo. We've gotten everything we need. Good day to you."

We departed the room and, after several minutes, the house. When Themus slammed the door behind us, Lockwood said, "The actor knows something."

"Lockwood, you cannot break into a townsperson's home like that. It's wrong, not to mention un-neighborly."

"Did you see the way he reacted when you spoke of the creature? His nostrils flared. Classic sign of a liar."

"Perhaps. Or perhaps he was upset about the giant mercenary woman breaking into his home and accusing him of stealing children at night. Or perhaps he was simply inhaling."

"Or…" The mercenary grinned and nodded. "He knows something. And I'm going to find out what."

The day had passed in a blink. Black shadows stretched across the white ground like patches of night. I shivered. I shivered again when I turned my gaze toward the Creaking Wood.

There was one more house yet before the forest. A small house, smaller even than the home of Pia's parents. Smoke billowed from the chimney.

"That's Murple's house," I said. "If anyone saw something, it would've been him."

"You think he saw your make-believe monster. Is that it?"

"The Megrim is very real, Lockwood. I assure you of that." I trudged forward, snow crunching beneath my boots. "You had your turn to investigate. Now let me have mine." I approached the house and knocked on the door.

No answer. I knocked again. "Mr. Murple, sir. Please, open the door. It's Pureman Wendyll. I need your assistance."

"Away with you," whispered a hushed voice from within. "I don't want to see you."

Lockwood lumbered forward and thumped on the door. I feared it might separate from its hinges. "I've already broken into one home today, villager, and your door looks rather flimsy."

I waved her off. "Mr. Murple. Please. We need your help. Did you see anything last night? Anything at all out of the ordinary?"

For a moment, there was no answer. Then a muffled sound passed through the door. I turned to Lockwood. "Is that…?"

"Sobbing," she said. "The man's sobbing."

"Mr. Murple, can you—"

The door whipped open. There he was, Murple himself, the old widower with the thick beard and the scarred forehead. He was the veteran of many battles, and he had the wounds to show for it. Yet now I was not paying attention to those. I only saw the fear in his eyes and the tears upon his cheeks.

"It's real," he whined. "It's real, it's there, I saw it. I saw it take her into the woods!"

"What's real?" I asked, dreading the answer. "What did you see?"

"I saw it!" Mr. Murple screamed. "It took her! The Megrim, Pureman. Goddess help us all, it was the Megrim!"

5

As Lockwood and I crept into the woods, my hands began to tremble. I tightened them into fists, the five fingers on my left and the two on my right. As we walked, I remembered again how these woods earned their name.

"Do you hear that, Lockwood?" I murmured. "It's as if…it sounds as if the trees are drawing nearer…" A breeze tugged on the bare branches. They creaked.

"Ah yes!" Lockwood chirped, pressing a cupped hand to her scarred ear. "I hear them, Pureman! They're flocking to tell me how boring they are. I agree with you, dear trees! You are indeed boring!"

I pulled my coat tighter, though it helped but little. Winter had come, and with it, the cold. "I wonder how woods could possibly be boring."

"These are. Where are the giant spiders, the walking fungi, the roving packs of man-eating bears? These woods only offer more trees and more snow. And so these woods are boring."

"I'd attribute them a different adjective."

"You of the obese vocabulary. What would you call them, then?"

Perhaps it would be unwise to voice my opinions on the woods. I doubted it would improve Lockwood's opinion of *me*, which I guessed was already quite low. Yet still, I was unaccustomed to withholding truths.

"Haunting," I said, "and vast. They cover most of the northern continent and stretch from one coast to the other. They run along the Ragman's Road toward the High Temple and beyond. Many a traveler has been lost within them, and many a folk tale warns of their watchful menace. It is said that smugglers used them to hide from bounty hunters. Some claim they built bunkers in the ground which lie hidden even today. But it's said other forgotten things are buried in the earth. And…"

"And…?"

I sniffled, exhaled, cleared my throat. "And, when I was no older than Pia, I went exploring in these woods. This was when my mother still lived, before I was an apprentice at the High Temple. I brought no books and no map. I wandered, just for the joy of wandering."

"That sounds unlike you, Pureman."

"I was not always averse to exploration—least of all when I was a child. As you might imagine, I lost my way. I found no familiar landmarks. Everything looked like everything else. Night descended, and I huddled among the trees, jumping at every creaking bough and snapping twig. Eyes watched me. Animal voices whispered in the dark. I did not sleep, but I did...I did cry.

"Late that night, a shape emerged from the woods. I have never known fear like that, Lockwood. It was like my entire body turned to ice, like all thought solidified into terror. The shape resembled a bird—but how could it be a simple bird? Gigantic it was, with stunted wings and legs like stone columns. It watched with eyes the color of bone, spoke with a beak that opened and closed but made no sound. It had a voice, but I did not hear it with my ears. Its words, somehow, were already inside my mind. Whatever it said, I could not comprehend it.

"I don't know what happened next. I awoke back home with my mother crying by my bedside. She told me my fellow people of Greengrove had formed a search party and found me. She said I'd nearly died of exposure. Compared to that, the three fingers I lost to frostbite seemed a small cost." I waggled the stumps, then smiled sadly. "I know what I saw. I know what saw me. It was the Megrim."

When I finished, the world seemed quieter than it had been. The only sound was the call of a crow somewhere in the distance.

And crying. Someone was crying. My eyes widened. It was Lockwood.

She stood with her back to me, framed by trees on

either side, great shoulders shuddering with her muffled sobs, axeheads clinking together softly. This I barely believed. The Lockwood I knew didn't seem the sort to weep over a childhood trauma. Yet here it was. I rushed to her side, placed a hand on her shoulder, whispered a soothing word and…and then I saw her face.

No tears. She was grinning. That's when I realized the truth. Those hadn't been stifled sobs. They were stifled laughs.

"What a bumbling *fool!*" she roared. "Wandering into the woods with no food nor water nor map, making a bed in the snow, then crying when things don't turn out well? Oh, that is *brilliant* planning, Pureman. Brilliant."

My face turned red. Worse, tears crept into my eyes. I walked away before she noticed. "I was only a boy," I said over my shoulder. "I was frightened."

That only made her laugh harder. She followed. "Well, Pureman, I've some news for you. I lost myself in the woods once, too, and I didn't go pissing myself or losing my fingers. It was the Forest of Dread down south—far larger and far more dangerous than this little garden. Went out hunting for a stag. My father told me I was not to hunt alone, but he was always too cautious. I tracked the beast through the brush and ended up lost, just like you. Spent two nights in the wild, though, not just the one."

I stepped over a deadfall and ducked beneath a set of clinging branches. "Were you saved?"

"Saved? You aren't saved in the Forest of Dread, Pureman. You're eaten, gored, or otherwise disemboweled by something bigger and hungrier than you. No, I found my own exit. Emerged on the western edge of the woods in some town I didn't know the name of."

"I am sorry. This forest must frighten you as much as me."

"Few things frighten me," she retorted, "and trees

aren't among them. So the following day, I went back in. You see, sometimes you need to get a little lost to learn your way around. I marched back into the Forest of Dread and I got what I came for. Returned home with the best venison anyone's ever eaten. A rack of antlers, too, though I couldn't eat those."

"An inspiring tale," I admitted. "Surely you kept the antlers as a mark of your victory."

Lockwood made a farting sound with her mouth. "Fuck victory. I sold 'em for gold and more food. Useful things, those." She stopped and knelt in the snow. "What have we here?"

I peered down where Lockwood stooped. "Those are tracks. Same as the ones at Pia's house. The tracks of the…"

"Megrim?" she snorted.

"Yes, that. How could they belong to anything else?"

"Tracks can be——"

"Easily faked. So you said."

Yet we followed them further, through a corridor of gnarled branches, up a slope, down the other side, over a toppled tree wrapped in fingerlike vines. The forest parted at the rise of a hill, offering our first unobstructed view of the sky since entering the woods. Gray was turning to black and the sun was an orange coin, sinking.

When I inspected the tracks again, my heart shuddered. "Look! These small tracks alongside the big ones. Those must be Pia's! She must be alive!" The imprints were clearly visible. One of a large birdlike sort, with seven toes on the left foot and six on the right. The other the small tread of a child's slipper.

Lockwood tucked a fist beneath her chin and whistled absently through a missing tooth. "Her captor must've carried her this far, then set her down to walk. Hardly the sign of a monster."

"What do you mean?"

"A creature like the Megrim, big and strong as it is, should be able to carry someone my size as far as it likes. A little girl it should carry farther. Why then did it put her down?"

That did seem odd. We walked deeper into the clearing, and there we found a single rotted tree stump. Spears were jammed into either side, giving it the look of a human with arms spread wide. Animal pelts hung from the spears and bird droppings covered the stump's surface. A coat of feathers stuck to the rest.

"This is evil work," I whispered. "Unholy. An altar of some fell design."

Lockwood frowned at it. "Yes. But an altar to what?"

The tracks became a confused jumble. The Megrim's clumped in a spot just before the trees resumed, and there something odd happened. They appeared to change. One track belonged to the Megrim. The next—something else.

"Tell me," Lockwood asked, "does that look like a boot print to you?"

Indeed it did. In one step, the Megrim's birdlike print changed into a plain old boot print.

"In your books, Pureman, have you seen mention of the Megrim changing from creature to human? Perhaps in the manner of the werewolf?"

"No. The Megrim has never been known to change form."

Lockwood followed the prints to a tree. She placed a foot into each track. Then she leaned against the trunk, raised one foot, and mumbled to herself. She mimed removing a shoe.

"I'm beginning to think," she said in a begrudging tone, "that we might've both been right about this case."

"How so?"

"You believe these children were taken by the Megrim.

I believe they were taken by someone from your village. Why not both? What if we're dealing with someone who has disguised themselves as the Megrim?"

A smile spread over my chapped lips. "A disguise. Yes. That's brilliant, Lockwood. When they want to be the Megrim, they don the costume. When they want to hide in plain sight, they remove it."

Shadows crept over the ground, draining the world's natural color. Snow descended from above. A cold wind whistled.

"They must be close." I cupped my hands around my mouth and bellowed. "Hello!? Pia! Children! Speak to us! Where are you?"

Lockwood crouched low and pushed aside frosted underbrush, cursing and scowling as she went. "Damn dark. Damn snow. I've lost the trail."

Daylight dwindled. Darkness spread. Snow fell. Tree branches creaked with the blowing wind. Off in the distance, an animal screeched. It had been cold before. But this? This was cold that could kill.

I felt like I was shrinking. My calls grew softer and softer until I said nothing at all. Pureman Wendyll was fading. I was regressing into the boy who'd been lost in the woods, the frightened child who could not find his way home. Lost, hopelessly lost, no way out and no one around to help. Only darkness, and something watching, watching, always watching...

I am ashamed to write what you will read next, yet I feel I must. I promised myself I'd give a fair and accurate account of what transpired. No author may shirk his responsibility to truth, no matter how damning it might be. So I shall spare no detail. I hope you will forgive me my shortcomings.

"Please, Lockwood," I whispered. "Can we turn back?"

She went rigid. "Turn back? What the hell do you mean, turn back?"

"We need to go home. It's too dark and too cold and I fear there's something…something out here with us…"

The mercenary gripped my arm. "The children must be nearby, Pureman. And my reward with them."

"Let us return in the morning," I begged. "Please. *Please.*" My voice took on a frantic whine. "I must…I must turn back…" I closed my eyes, and when I opened them I found myself seated upon the snow, my bottom all wet and frigid. I huddled into a ball, small as I could make myself, and there I sat, rocking back and forth, pleading.

"I want that money, Pureman. Now you'll either get up and walk, or you'll stay here and you'll truly be alone. The choice is yours."

Snowflakes settled upon me. I had to escape, yet I couldn't stand, I couldn't walk, I couldn't do anything but shiver.

"Fine then. Stay here." She paced off into the brush.

I wept, trembled, hid my face with my hands. I know not how much time passed. Hours, perhaps, though how many, I could not say. My senses froze. My world became fear.

And then a hand touched my shoulder. A familiar voice said, "By my breakfast, Pureman. When I said I was leaving, I thought you'd follow me."

I looked up. There stood Lockwood the mercenary, her scarred face barely visible in the twilight. She looked almost—I couldn't believe it—almost concerned. Yet the expression dissipated in an instant, replaced by her familiar scowl. "On your feet, you pansy." She offered me a hand. "You'll freeze if you sit there." She pulled, but I could not stand. She pulled again.

"I…Lockwood, I…"

"There's nothing more we can do tonight. I've lost the

trail and there's no light to see by. You were right. We must turn back."

I tried to rise, yet my body would not allow it. "Lockwood, I…I think my legs might have…fallen off."

Her snort clapped through the quiet. "Then what are those trembling stalks attached to your torso, eh? Do they work?"

My teeth chattered too vigorously to answer. I suppose that was answer enough.

"Very well, then." With no more effort than a parent lifting a child, she hoisted me onto her shoulders. "Tell no one of this. I'm warning you, Pureman. I've a reputation to uphold."

I tried to respond, but no words passed my frozen lips.

"Save your strength. Tomorrow, we must find ourselves a guide…"

Consciousness gave way to cold. The world turned black.

6

I awoke the following morning feeling ashamed. My shame quickly snapped into panic.

I sprang from my bed, pulled on the clothes closest to hand, tugged my boots onto my feet, all the while recalling the events of the previous night. How I'd wept, how I'd ruined what might've been our only chance of finding the children again. It was enough to make me well and truly hate myself.

"I'm sorry, children," I said to the dawn. "I'll find you. I'll save you all."

But how? We'd found the altar they'd been taken to, yet still no children. All we had was a cryptic observation from

Lockwood: *"What if we're dealing with someone who has disguised themselves as the Megrim?"*

But how could anyone do such a thing? And for what purpose?

The Goddess teaches self-love and realization of inner worth, yet still I could not force the shame from my mind. My guilt was a stain, my soul the soiled cloth. I hurried out into the morning.

It appeared no additional snow had fallen overnight. That was a rarity, especially for this winter. I scuffled along the walkway and onto our town's main path. Lockwood. Where was Lockwood?

After a half hour of searching, I found her sprawled out in the stables. She slept upon no mattress and had no pillow, save for a bundle of rags. She appeared to be having a very fine dream. I tapped her shoulder. "Lockwood. We have work to do."

She slept on. I tried nudging harder, then shaking her. Still she did not wake.

Fear not, dear reader. She wasn't dead. In fact, she snored titanically through my entire effort. It seemed, rather, that she was an obstinate sleeper.

After several more fruitless attempts, I finally opted for a high-pitched scream. (My voice can grow quite shrill when the situation calls for it.) This one worked. The woman sat bolt upright, her forehead stopping within inches of mine. "Dammit, Pureman. Couldn't you just nudge me?"

I bowed my head. "I must apologize for my…my cowardice yesterday. And I owe you thanks for saving my life. Thank you, Lockwood. Now I ask you one more favor. We must go back. We must find the children."

Lockwood yawned and launched herself from the ground. "Apology accepted, Pureman. Being scared shitless every now and then reminds us we're alive. Anyway, returning to the Boring Woods does no good. They're too vast. We could waste days finding and losing the trail. We need a better strategy."

"You spoke of a guide last night, did you not?"

"Aye."

"But the woodsmen travel rarely in the winter. I've not seen one since fall."

"Not that sort of guide. I mean the one who knows where they are. The one who took them."

"The captor shall lead us to the captured. Yes." I pursed my lips. "I've been thinking on what you said. Someone who thinks they're the Megrim. Someone who's disguised themselves. But who would...?" The answer parted my sorrow like a ray of dawn's light through clouds. "A disguise. Tell me, who in this town is most likely to pretend at anything? A performer, Lockwood. An *actor*. Lendo. It must be Lendo the Versatile."

"I told you he flared his nostrils." Lockwood sighed. "Am I meant to be amazed by your work, Pureman? I'm only amazed you took this long to figure it out. I came to that conclusion hours ago."

"Ah. Very good, then." I tipped my head back in thought. "Yet why would Lendo kidnap children? He's a man of Greengrove. He's owned a home here for years. I can't believe a citizen of our town would do something so heinous."

"Perhaps he'll explain it to us." With that, Lockwood cracked her knuckles and marched outside. I followed.

When we arrived at the front door of Lendo the Versatile's mansion, Lockwood pounded it several times. "Open up, actor! By decree of me, drag your gilded ass out of bed and answer us!"

She kept on banging until a panel slid open on the door. Two eyes stared out, bleary from sleep. "Have you any idea what time it is, woman? Master Lendo must needs get his 14 hours of rest, elsewise he cannot perform."

"Themus," I pleaded, "we must speak with Lendo. The matter is urgent."

Lockwood had a less tactful way of putting things. "Open this door, manservant, or I'll be smashing it down upon your head."

Themus's eyes narrowed. "You will leave now, or else—"

The mercenary moved so quickly I might've missed it had I blinked. Her hand darted toward the open panel and, her pointer and middle fingers forming a V-shape, she jabbed both of Themus's eyes. The man squealed in pain and vanished from sight. "She poked me!" he screeched. "The wench poked me!"

"Aye. Now let's poke this door."

Lockwood spat and drew one of her axes. I hadn't realized how long they were until that moment: four and a half feet from top to bottom. And the blade of the weapon...I was beginning to understand why she was so feared in the stories.

Three chops was all it took. The first split the door like a ram through glass. The second dislodged it and left it dangling from the topmost hinge. The third wasn't even necessary.

Once finished, Lockwood stowed her axe and stepped over the ruin of the door. "Poke," she said.

The mansion was empty. Themus was nowhere to be seen, yet his bawling carried through the vast hallways. We strode through them, Lockwood and I. Though we'd just broken into the home of the richest man in Greengrove, my anticipation exceeded my fright. I sensed we were drawing close now, close to the truth. And so we strode.

On the third floor we found a luxurious bedroom, within which sat a woman on a four-poster bed. She wore a golden necklace and nothing else. I recognized her immediately: the harpist from the previous day.

"He's under there," she said, pointing downward.

Lockwood reached beneath the bed and yanked out a squirming man. Lendo the Versatile, just as naked as his companion. His sniveling and whimpering reminded me of a lamb that knows it's about to be slaughtered. "You can't kill me. Please. Kill me and you kill the arts."

"Did you take them?" I bellowed. The sound of my own voice frightened me. "Was it you, Lendo? Did you do it?"

"Take who? I—"

Lockwood gave him a slap. "The children, you oaf. Where are they? You lied to us about them, you lied to us about the Megrim. Tell us where they are."

"The Megrim? There is no Megrim, it's only a myth, a role, a costume..." His words dissolved into a puddle of sobs.

"Costume?" Lockwood shook him. "Speak!"

"A costume!" he screamed. "For my next role, my greatest challenge as an actor yet. I've played humans all, both fictional and historical. But to play a monster—it's the performance my career needs."

"So you're the Megrim."

"Only for the production—for theater! My costume was made by the finest designer in the land. Incredibly life-like. I needed to understand the creature, to get inside its mind. 'Method acting,' the theorists call it. I wore the costume about the mansion every night, to get into character."

Lockwood loomed over the blubbering man with all the presence of a grizzly bear. "You admit it, then? You admit you dressed as the Megrim and kidnapped the children?"

Lendo's handsome face looked a deal less so with snot

oozing over his lips. "No, I—no, no, no, you do not understand. My costume—someone stole it! I know not who. I kept it in the closet, er, one of the closets. Someone stole it from me! Yes, I withheld the truth, I admit it! But it's only because I knew you'd never believe me. I feared you'd accuse me anyway, even though I did nothing wrong. You must listen to me, Pureman. My costume was stolen!"

Lockwood opened her mouth to speak, then hesitated. She glanced at me. "Do you hear something?"

I did. At first I thought it was the drawn note of a horn, one elongated blast echoing through the still air outside. But no. Not a horn. A voice. One word amplified to a frenzied pitch.

"Gone!" the voice keened. "Gooooonnnnneee!"

Lockwood stuck a finger in Lendo's face. "Don't go anywhere." She stuffed him back under the bed and together we hurried outside, down the entryway stairs, and onto the town's main road. A man huddled on the ground before us, a trembling lump in the snow.

Faces emerged from homes and shops. I knew them all: Murple, Asrith, Glendon Glubb, the Lobells. We gathered around the whimpering man, one unspoken question lingering on our tongues.

I was the first to find my voice. "Who? Who is gone?"

"My son." The man raised his head and I knew him instantly: Piebald. The cobbler. "My son Lommy. Gone in the night. Taken by…by…" His lips curled. "Why didn't you save him, Wendyll? Your High Pureman promised to help. But what has he done to help us? What have *you* done?"

"I…we…"

"There were tracks!" Piebald screamed, springing to his feet. "Tracks in the snow by Lommy's window, vanishing into the woods. Seven toes on the left foot, six on the right!"

A ripple of uneasy chatter swept through the towns-people. Two stepped forward: Lara and Lorn. Pia's parents.

"The same creature took our girl," said Lara, barely loud enough to hear. "Tracks of seven and six."

"I saw it!" came another voice. It was Murple, pushing through the throng and waving his arms like a man over-board. "Outside my home! The Megrim it was, the Megrim!"

That word killed the chatter. Murple leveled one outstretched finger at me. "I told him. Him and his husky woman there. And what did they do? Nothing! They did nothing!"

"Husky, am I?" Lockwood reached for an axe, but I held her arm. Murple carried on as if oblivious.

"They go into the woods and return with *nothing*. And meanwhile, the monster takes another little one!"

"Patience, my dear friends," I said, "you must have patience, please! We are conducting an investigation. We will find your children, I'm certain we will. They are not lost. We aren't even sure we're dealing with the Megrim here."

"But I *saw* it!" Murple screeched.

My response was lost in the ensuing tumult. Cries of "The Megrim!" and "Save our children!" erupted from the crowd. They pressed forward and closed in.

"The High Temple has forsaken us!"

"We must slay it! We must slay the monster!"

"Save the children! Save them!"

A woman shoved through the townsfolk and called for silence. It was granted in an instant. She had red hair bunched beneath a dull cloth, sleeves rolled up to show bloody forearms. Bregna. The town butcher.

"You all know me," she said. "You all know my daughter Zel. She's been gone almost a week now. I don't know if she's live or dead, but I've tried makin' my peace either way." Her voice cracked and she paused before continuing. "Now what I want is answers. And if it comes to it, vengeance. We ain't gettin' either from them two, so I says we get 'em ourselves."

Vengeance. If ever there was a word to stir up a mob, that was it. These townspeople I had known so well, builders and cobblers and tradespeople and honest good folk all, they didn't seem that way anymore. Now they seemed more like a rabble. Like monsters themselves.

Bregna the Butcher roared, "We'll meet by my shop at midday. Arm yourselves with whatever you got. We ain't waitin' for the Temple no longer. The High Pureman and his bitch-Goddess can go fuck each other, for all I care." She glared at me when she said that. "Who's joining?"

And to my horror, a thunderous roar erupted from my fellow villagers. Such gentle people they had been only hours ago. What terrible things parents will do for the lives of their children.

"Wait!" I shouted. "Please! My friends, hear me. We still don't know what's out there. We must trust in the agent the High Pureman has sent us."

It didn't help that Lockwood chose that moment to munch noisily upon a loaf of bread she'd conjured from nowhere. "Hmm?" she mumbled around a mouthful.

"Or...or...if not her, trust in *me*. I am your friend, dear people. I sent to the Temple for aid. I've done everything I can to find your sons and daughters. Do you not trust me? Do you not know that I am your friend?"

A long silence followed that question. Snow had begun to fall, puffy flakes that stuck to my cheeks and melted like tears.

"Pureman," Piebald said, his voice little more than a whisper, "how can I trust you? You let this creature take my boy. And now he might be...Lommy might be..." His words became sobs. He turned his back on me. One by one, the other townspeople did the same.

"Wait!" I said. "Let me come with you. Let me help you!"

Bregna the Butcher shook her head. "Stay here, Pureman. You'll only slow us down and get yourself lost, like you did all those years ago. You're no investigator. Just stay here. Read your books."

No more words were spoken. None needed to be. The mob dispersed and left me there with Lockwood. She finished her bread, then turned.

"Not you, too."

"What? Did you think I'd move in?"

"I thought we'd finish this together. That we'd save those children. It's only been a day."

Lockwood peered off at the trees. "It's been more than a week for some of them, Pureman. There's likely no one left to save. This mob of yours will find that out soon enough."

"But the costume. The tracks. We're so close."

Lockwood only shrugged. "Close doesn't get me my remaining money. Your Temple already paid me half. The other would come from solving the case, and that won't be happening now. Who covers more area: a mercenary and a holy man, or an entire town?"

"Lockwood," I whispered, failing to withhold the pleading note in my voice. "I need your help. The children need your help."

"The children are dead, Pureman. Killed by some lunatic wearing a bird costume. Best I cut my losses and get moving."

"Can't you bring yourself to care about anything besides money?" I asked. "Anything besides yourself?"

She never answered me. When I looked up, she was gone.

I retreated to my quarters and barred the door. I grew hungry and my clothes grew stale, yet I didn't move. I couldn't. My village didn't want me anymore. Nairn Lockwood had abandoned us. I had failed.

In hindsight, I suppose I could've been less melodramatic. I do not consider myself one of those morose, doomsaying holy men. But I was hurt, and I believe rightly so. I rose from my bed only to relieve myself and only to take the occasional glance from my window. All I saw was falling snow.

"Goddess," I said as I stared at the ceiling, "give them the wisdom to find what I could not. Help them save Halfmoon and Zel and Lommy and Pia. Keep the children safe. And above all, I beg you…ask them to forgive me. I did all I could do."

Yet the Goddess, as she so often does, offered no reply.

I had fitful dreams while I slept. Dreams of monsters in the woods, of a play in which all the actors were corpses of children, of Nairn Lockwood melting like ice in spring, of library books opening their jaws and biting me, devouring me, digesting me…

I read and reread stories of the Megrim. *A stalker of dreams. A collector of small creatures. A chief among birds.* An entity that did not exist. The Megrim was a man in a costume, just as Lockwood theorized.

Yet if that was true, what had I seen in the woods so long ago? I had no answer.

The following day I noticed my book was due back at the library. I imagined Asrith's crinkled face, her cracked fingernails clacking on the countertop. *Is there a Goddess of Tardiness, Pureman? If so, you must be her favorite follower.*

I might've laughed under other circumstances. Yet still, the thought of Asrith gave me hope. She was hard on me, yes, but in a motherly sort of way. Asrith was an old friend. Asrith was a reader. And one can always benefit from a reader's counsel. I stepped out into the day, books in hand.

Frigid winds jabbed my cheeks. I yanked my hood over my head and pulled it tight. I took a step, nearly toppled over a titanic drift. It must've snowed all night. Onward. I pushed through the snow and headed for the library.

Along the way I saw no one. An eerie effect, to be sure; most of the town must've joined the coalition, or had otherwise stayed indoors. I found myself praying they were warm and safe, wherever they were. I hoped they were alright.

The ice coating the library made it look like a bear in hibernation. Smoke rose from the cinder chimney. I stepped inside.

"Is that a Pureman I see?" Asrith sat behind the counter, reading as usual. "I told you not to be late with those books."

"Not late. Only *almost* late. Do you have any warmth to spare?"

"Some. Could use more." Aside from Asrith, I didn't know anyone who could be both gruff and kindly in the same breath. "You caused quite an uproar, Pureman. You're the first person I've seen all day."

"They're hunting the Megrim, aren't they?"

"Vigorously. Some have returned, most not. Give a mob a good monster and they'll be occupied for days."

I set my books upon the counter. Asrith flipped through them, marking them once on her crumbling catalog, then again inside the books themselves.

"Asrith," I asked. "Have I failed them?"

The old librarian didn't often laugh, but she did at that. "As an investigator? Certainly. But as a Pureman? Never."

Asrith's quill flicked across the catalog. "Our little village is quaint, yes. But sometimes you speak of its people like they're divine. They're not. They're just people."

"I don't understand."

Asrith sighed. "Listen, Wendyll. You did your damnedest. If anyone ostracizes you, it's because they're frightened, not because you didn't do enough. It isn't fair, but it's human nature. They fear for their children, and that fear has turned them desperate and cruel." She ran a dry tongue over chapped lips. "I'm sorry. I'm not much for words. I prefer reading them, not making them myself."

"No need for apologies. Not when you're right."

"I'm always right. Haven't you noticed that by now?" She checked off the remaining volumes. "Now for this old woman's least favorite job…"

"Allow me." I scooped the books and slipped between the shelves. "Anything I can do to help."

"I don't need help," Asrith growled. Yet she didn't say no. Instead, she pointed to another stack in the corner. "But if you insist, shelve those too. Good lad."

I set to work returning the books to their proper places. I dared not stare at the volume about the Megrim too long —if I did, I knew it would spoil what little good humor I'd regained by coming here. I stuffed it onto its shelf, did the same with the rest. Only one book remained.

It was a beaten old husk that resembled a dried plant more than a book. It was so worn that the leather cover seemed to curl in on itself. The ink of the title had all but faded, yet still I discerned the outline of the words: *Ancient Gods of the Deep Woods*. I brought the book back to the counter.

"Asrith. What's this? I've never seen it before."

"That's because it's not ours. I procured it on loan from a library down south."

Delicately, I tilted back the cover and ran my thumb

over the pages. A thought occurred to me. I opened to the index and scanned the list until I found the subject I'd been looking for. Page 876. I flipped to it and read.

The Nameless Prince of Snows, Nemesis of the Goddess and Bringer of the Black Morning, is known to possess countless minions and followers. The raven is his servant, and the woodpecker and the thrush and the crow are said to whisper his name when human ears are absent.

More or less standard procedure for evil gods. But the next line turned my skin to gooseflesh.

It is whispered that his most prized servant is the Lord of Birds itself: The Megrim.

The Nameless Prince of Snows treasures sacrifice above all else. He reveals himself only when the moon is quarter-full, for the quarter moon reflects his number, which is four. When four lives are offered, it is said one can hear his call in the distance. He shall come only for the loyal Megrim, and only when the proper sacrifices have been assembled. When he arrives he shall assimilate his snows and his offerings, and all shall be barren and dry as he spreads his thousand wings.

Yet it is said sacrifice and timing alone are not enough. The Nameless Prince's Song must be sung, and its words are

I turned to the next page; it was a new chapter on world origin stories. I flipped back, checked the page number, then checked the number on the one following.

"This book," I whispered, "is missing a page."

"Poor thing." Asrith patted it as if it was an arthritic old cat. "Ancient volume, older even than me. Only just returned."

"Who, Asrith? Who returned the book?"

"I'm not supposed to tell you that." Yet she shrugged

and inspected her catalog all the same. "Looks like it was Mr. Glubb."

Glendon Glubb. A citizen of our town for years. Could it be?

I dashed out the door. "Thank you, Asrith," I called over my shoulder. "Best librarian in the world! Thank you! *Thank you!*"

Back to my quarters I flew, snow swirling all around. I leapt over a drift, lost my footing, rolled, then sprang to my feet and ran onward. Afternoon was already upon us. I had to make haste. The children would—

I thudded against something and went sprawling. Not something, I realized. Some*one*.

"Would you believe it, Pureman? Yesterday I ran into somebody, now somebody runs into me. Perhaps the world is telling me something."

He wore a thick coat and puffy mittens that made his hands appear disproportionately large. A scarf hid half his face, yet I could tell by his eyes he was smiling. He stood and offered a hand.

Glendon Glubb. The builder.

I ignored his hand and hauled myself to my feet. "Mr. Glubb. What brings you outside on a wintry afternoon like this?"

"Searching for our dear children, of course. The Goddess knows we need them." The picture of a concerned neighbor. "But alas, no sign. We checked for miles around, and nothing. I fear the worst."

"I don't. I'm quite certain they're alive, and still out there."

Glubb brushed snow from his coat. "I admire your optimism. But why so sure?"

"Faith." I didn't want the man to know what I knew— yet the reckless spirit awoken inside me thought otherwise. "Have you read any good books lately, Mr. Glubb?"

"Several. Not so many as you, I'm sure, but several, yes."

"Perhaps you'd recommend one to me. Sometimes the right book is so hard to find."

The man was a fine liar. The corners of his mouth poked above the scarf. "And where are you off to, Pureman, on a frigid afternoon like this?"

"Into the forest. To find the children."

"A brave gesture, but futile. Some of us searched all night. I came back to sleep, then resumed this morning. Didn't matter. This Megrim, whatever it is, it's claimed them. I fear we won't get them back."

"I think not," I said, restraining the accusation that fluttered behind my lips. "I'm going to find them."

"And what if the Megrim finds you first?"

"Then I'll fight it."

Glubb sputtered with laughter. "You? Fight? Wendyll, the only fighter in this town was that hungry woman you recruited, and I don't see her around. What makes you think you can do better?"

"Nothing," I said. "I don't believe I have any chance at all. But I'm going anyway."

That silenced his laughter. "These snows, Pureman. They're bad for the mind. They make people do irrational things." He clasped my shoulder and squeezed. Hard. "Don't be irrational. Never know what you might run into on a night like tonight." And with a final squeeze, he left me there.

I didn't hesitate. I barreled into my quarters and donned my warmest furs and boots. It would be cold, perhaps colder even than last night.

I waited by my window and watched as the remaining searchers filed in from the woods, wet and shivering. They vanished into their homes, one by one, and soon none remained. All the while, snow drifted down from above.

The children were still out there, I had no doubt. But they wouldn't be found—not unless the person who hid them showed the way. I needed a guide, as Lockwood had said. And so I would have one.

I waited until dusk, when the lights of the world flickered low and the shadows of the houses turned twisted and strange. I slipped from my quarters and crept toward Glubb's house, all the while fearing how terribly quiet and empty it was. I hid beneath the shadow of his neighbor's home and waited.

Time passed. Snow fell. Night descended. The moon rose. And Glubb's door creaked open.

He emerged wearing a traveler's cloak with the hood pulled over his face. He carried a heavy sack over his shoulder. The fire still burned in his home—a likely explanation of his whereabouts, should anyone wonder where he'd been.

Glubb glared around in all directions. Then he set off into the woods.

I waited, waited, listening only to the rhythm of my own pulse. I counted to 100. Then I followed.

His tracks were cloaked in darkness and already filling with fresh snow, yet I managed to follow nonetheless. I crept as quietly as I could, for I did not fear being seen anymore—I feared being *heard*.

At times I spotted Glubb up ahead. If he halted for even a moment, he'd likely hear me and the pursuit would be for naught. But the Goddess was present, it seemed—or more likely, time was against him. Tonight was the night of the quarter moon. He hurried ahead, never stopping.

I cannot say how long I pursued him. Hours, though I know not how many. Twice I thought I heard something behind me, perhaps even a human voice, but I walked onward. My will was adamant.

Moonlight illuminated a clearing in the trees and

turned the snow silver. The sight put me in mind of horror stories I'd found at the library and read under candlelight. I clamped my jaw shut, fearful that my chattering teeth might spoil my secrecy.

Glubb stepped into the light of the clearing and approached something standing in the middle of it: The odd shrine, the one Lockwood and I had discovered when we'd first entered the forest and followed the tracks. Its feathers fluttered in the wind.

Glubb set down his sack and whispered to the shrine. I wanted to rush at him, tackle him, hit him. I'd never felt the urge to hurt anyone, but in that moment, I did. Yet I could do nothing until he revealed the children. Where were they?

He stepped further into the trees, further even than Lockwood and I had gone two nights prior. Here the branches grew wild and thick, clinging and scratching like grasping talons. I kept my distance, knowing that if I cut through the clearing and Glubb doubled back, he'd spot my tracks.

We carried on like this for another handful of minutes, Glubb pushing through branches and me following from afar. He turned and began walking...

Toward me. Straight toward me. A calm approach, nothing hasty, and for a moment, my heart froze. My eyes snapped open, my mouth locked into a grimace. I thought I'd been hidden by the skeletal underbrush, yet that now appeared false. He drew a knife from beneath his coat.

He came within seven strides of me. Six. Five.

Glubb stooped and brushed a lump of dead branches aside. He appeared to be tracing a line on the ground. His hand searched the snow and came away with something: a chain. He tugged on it, growled, tugged again.

It was a door, I realized. A trapdoor built into the

ground itself. Glubb strained, pulled, cursed, and finally the door swung open with the crunch of breaking ice.

It was just as my books had said. Smugglers in these woods and their hidden bunkers. Glubb had found one. All this time we'd been looking for the children, and they were just beneath our feet.

From where I hid, I could see only the top of the open door—nothing within. Yet I heard them. They were crying.

"Good evening, little ones," said Glendon Glubb, waving the knife. "Out with you now. Out."

They came quietly. All four of them, each with their hands tied behind their backs and their wrists strung together. First came Halfmoon, the boy who'd first gone missing. It had been more than a week since I'd last seen him. A wolf pelt hanging around his shoulders slipped off, and he shivered violently. Next came Zel, the butcher's daughter, tears frozen to her cheeks. And then came Lommy, Piebald's boy, the one taken most recently. He blinked and stared about with wide eyes.

And finally, Pia. My apprentice. She was the eldest of the four and it showed. Her mouth was set in a determined line, her fists clenched behind her back. She glared at Glubb with a hatred I'd never seen in her eyes.

All four children. Alive.

"Walk," Glubb ordered, "but don't run. Please. You won't get far, what with all this snow… "

They stumbled ahead in single file. I followed. When they reached the clearing, Glubb tethered the children to a tree trunk. He then dug into the sack he'd brought with him and produced a mass of dark fabric. Incredibly lifelike. It took him several minutes to don the thing. The children shivered, watching in mesmerized dread.

When he finished, he said, "Behold. The Megrim."

I must admit—I thought seeing that horrible creature

once again would bring me fear. I thought stepping back into childhood, becoming the little boy I'd been once again, I thought that might revive my terror. It didn't.

Lendo the Versatile's costume was convincing, it must be said. He'd spoken so highly of its quality, and in that he was correct. Glubb appeared completely transformed: He was now a gigantic black bird, wings tucked into his sides, massive eyes staring wide and white, snub beak clacking open and shut.

A fine costume. Yet a costume nonetheless. Was this what I saw in the woods all those years ago? A man in an outfit? I could not say. For now, I could only watch, and creep closer.

Glubb's arms protruded from beneath the folded wings of his costume, his face from above the beak. He took the children by the shoulders, gently, then guided them each to a tree at the edge of the clearing. He untethered them from one another and bound their hands to branches; Zel and Halfmoon, the younger of the two children, wept as he did it. The boy Lommy seemed unable to comprehend what was happening. Which left only one. Pia.

Glubb trudged toward her. "You'd best not try to bite me again, young lady."

"Certainly not," she answered.

Glubb took her by the wrists, and suddenly she roared and dealt him a savage kick between his legs. It was delivered with enough force to double him up—or would have been, had he not been wearing the costume. It appeared to absorb most of the blow.

"That wasn't a bite," said Pia.

Glubb snatched her by the arm and yanked her toward a tree. Mustering all my courage, I stepped into the clearing.

"Stop, Glendon. In the name of Greengrove, stop this."

Glubb studied me. Even beneath his costume, his presence filled the clearing with menace. I'd never thought of him like that before. He'd always been so warm, so unassuming. He'd always been the man who fixed roofs in wintertime, sometimes for no pay at all. He'd always been a fellow reader, a man who read at night by firelight. He'd always been worthy of trust. Lockwood's words echoed in my mind: *"I believe we're looking for someone from your town, likely an older, charming presence. Someone others admire and respect."*

"Wendyll," Glubb said. "I thought I told you not to do anything irrational." He held Pia between us, grasping her by the hair.

"Why?" I demanded. My breath billowed in a fog before me. My teeth chattered. My fists, both the whole left and partial right, clenched and unclenched. "Why do this? How could you? They're only children."

"Indeed they are. Good little children. I invited them to the woods and they came, all four of them. It was only me, after all, kind old Mr. Glubb. I told them I had a friend who could grant them a wish. And they liked my costume."

"You stole it. From Lendo."

"Wasn't difficult. I'd been hired to make additions to his home, and one day he brags about his new costume, a certain mythical bird. He likes to brag, our Lendo. So I snuck into his closet and took it for myself, threw it into my sack, went home. Easy as that."

"How could you steal from him? He's your fellow villager."

Glubb's costume shifted, perhaps due to a shrug from inside. "He'll understand. Our village is so *lonely*."

"It's home."

"If you say so. I believe it's lonely, and cold, and buried in snow. Like a corpse. It's just as I told you, Wendyll.

These snows…they're unnatural. We need someone to clean them up."

"Glendon," I said. "This is not the way. The snows will thaw. The spring will come."

"Will it? I wish I could be as certain as you. I cannot. I see a winter without end. I see snow and ice and chilling wind. I believe we need help. He will come for his favored servant, and for his four sacrifices, and for his words."

At this I could no longer stand idly. I rushed forward, weaponless, knowing not what I'd do when I reached the man, knowing only that I *had* to reach him, stop him. He drew a tattered paper from within his costume—it had to be the page that was missing from the book. And with his other hand, he drew the knife. He pressed it to Pia's throat.

"That's far enough."

I fell to my knees. "Stop, Glendon! Stop this!"

Yet Glubb only shook his head. "Don't you see what I'm doing? I'm saving us. I'm drawing off the snows."

I began a retort, yet Pia spoke faster. "It's alright, Pureman Wendyll. The Goddess will melt him to jelly, you'll see."

I wished I could share her optimism. As a Pureman of the High Temple, I should have believed in Her power. I should have raised my head to the stars and known that the Goddess would descend and save us.

No. There would be no divine intervention here. Someone had to do something. But what more could I do?

Glendon Glubb sang from his paper. The words were unfamiliar, yet he used them with confidence and accuracy. They sounded ancient, caustic, venomous. Words not meant to be sung by human tongues.

A line of dark blood ran down Pia's throat. If I came any closer, he'd kill her. Was the Goddess truly our only hope?

The singing ceased. Glubb grinned triumphantly,

tossed the paper aside. The children whimpered. Not Pia, though—she remained stony-faced. If only I could have her strength.

Seconds turned to minutes. No wind, no sound of forest creatures. But for the sobs of the children, there was no sound at all.

"Hello?" Glubb called. Was that fear in his voice? "My Prince? Hello? Perhaps you'd like me to try again? I could sing it louder this time—or, or slower. I've brought you everything you wanted. The blood of these children is yours to drink, the snow of this village yours to consume. Lift the winter, oh holy and nameless one. Please. Save us!"

A twig snapped behind us. My heart lurched. I wheeled, expecting to see some demonic entity lumbering through the woods. Instead, a red blur whizzed past my head.

It moved too fast for my eyes to follow. Yet when I turned back to Glubb, I heard a sound like a wet cloth striking a wall. He yelped, and something exploded upon his forehead. It came to rest in the snow before his feet.

An apple.

The knife came loose of Pia's throat, and she took her opportunity. She drove her heel into Glubb's toes, then slammed her head into his mouth. He screeched and tumbled backward, his feet slipping on ice, his limbs flailing, and he toppled to the ground, yelping like a wounded animal. Pia snatched up the knife and cut her wrists free, then ran to the other children and sawed at their bonds.

I leapt over the struggling form of Glendon Glubb and dashed to Lommy. "He promised me happiness," the boy blubbered. "He promised me I'd get to meet God." I untied him. By then Pia had freed Halfmoon and Zel. The five of us huddled together, myself in front and the children behind.

"I'm sorry, Pureman Wendyll," Pia said. "I only

followed him so I could save the others. I thought I could fight him, but with the knife...he threatened the children, and..."

"It's alright, Pia," I said. "It's alright now." To Glubb, I called, "You will not harm them, Glendon."

I must say, the man looked pitiful as he rolled in the snow. His stolen costume was twisted around so that his shoulder poked out the face hole. The beak was bent the wrong way. He stood, wobbled. "Who threw that? Who threw it? Which one of you brats was it?"

"Not them," boomed a voice from the trees. "Me."

A woman entered the clearing. She wore travel-stained clothes and held two massive axes, one to each hand. She grinned, revealing several missing teeth.

"My name is Nairn Lockwood," she roared, "and I'm hungry. I'll be needing my apple back."

A grin parted my lips. We hadn't gotten the Goddess. But at that moment, Nairn Lockwood was the next best thing.

"No." Glubb's words began as a whisper, then built to a gibbering scream. "No. No no no no no no *no!* I did everything you asked, my Prince! I gathered your sacrifices and I spoke your words and I arrived here on your night! I came in the guise of your favored servant! Everything was here, everything you require! You've abandoned me, oh Prince! You've abandoned us to the snow, you've—!"

A sound from above. A rustling of wings. A shape passed before the quarter-moon, then descended. It settled upon Glubb's shoulder.

"Lockwood," I called. I edged around the clearing, nudging the children to follow me. I remained between them and Glubb. The problem was, Glubb stood between Lockwood and us. To go anywhere but back where we'd come would only draw us further into the woods. "Lockwood, we must flee. There's something foul afoot."

"You came," Glubb said to the shape on his shoulder. It was a bird. A crow. "You answered my call. I knew you would." A second bird descended from the sky, this one a thrush, and settled upon his other shoulder. A woodpecker sat upon his head. A raven joined them.

Lockwood laughed. "This is nothing, Pureman. Merely a flock of birds."

"No." I edged closer to her. "This is something far worse."

By now an entire swarm had settled upon Glendon Glubb. He stretched his arms outward, looking just like the altar behind him, and more birds perched upon him.

"Yes!" he cackled. "Yes, yes, you have heard me, you have heard my prayer!"

He laughed and he screamed, and soon it became impossible to discern one from the other. His body was covered in birds, all except his face. He opened his mouth to laugh again, and—

"Goddess," I moaned. "Look away, children. Look *away.*" I realized only later that telling children to avert their eyes is more likely to have the opposite effect. Still, I believe they obeyed my command. I hope they did. For I wish I had done the same.

When Glubb opened his mouth, the crow burrowed inside him. It tucked its wings in and, like a gopher down a hole, it wiggled between his lips and into his throat. The bird was too wide to fit neatly, so it stretched and split Glubb's cheeks at either corner. He made a horrible stran- gled sound while the bird's feet kicked against his tongue and the roof of his mouth. His eyes bulged and whirled wildly. When they settled on me, I covered my face. When I dared look again, Glubb was laughing. Goopy blood clung to his chin.

"I am…ha ha…I am blessed…ha ha…I am blessed… "

The thrush wedged itself down his throat next, and that was enough. We scampered across the clearing, the children and I, passing Glubb and stopping at Lockwood's side. "We must go. We must return to the village."

The mercenary's eyes remained fixed on Glubb, and the birds engulfing him. "Go, then. I'd like to give my axes some exercise."

I pulled her arm but it was like tugging on a stone wall. "Lockwood, listen to me. Whatever's happening here is nothing you can fight. This is a deity, a creature of another world. Blades cannot cleave it. Weapons cannot harm it."

"Perhaps not. But when you return to your village, where then will you go? It will follow. And you'll have no weapon to defend yourself with. Luckily for me," and she hefted both axes, grinning, "I have two."

"Lockwood—"

"I am Nairn Lockwood, Pureman Wendyll, and I am ordering you to save those children. Will you deny me?"

I studied the children. They looked cold and frightened and traumatized (all but Pia, of course, who appeared only furious). The Goddess says we all have parts to play in this world. The teacher must practice pedagogy. The artist must make good art. The fighter must fight. And the Pureman...

"Goddess defend you, Lockwood," I said. "You are the bravest person I've ever met."

"You're fucking right on that score. Now if I die here, Wendyll...tell the story. And make sure it's a damn good one."

"I promise it. Goodbye, my friend."

I gathered the children and we ran. I followed at their backs, making sure all four stayed together, that we would lose none of them. I managed one last glimpse over my shoulder as we fled. The mass of birds had grown even thicker. They still clung to Glubb's body, forming a conglomerate humanoid mass of writhing wings. The eeriest part, though, was that the birds were silent. No caws, no shrieks. Only the rustle of feathers.

Then came a voice. It originated from Glendon Glubb but it was not his own. It was thunderous, primal, and chilling, all at once. I know not what it said, but I'll never forget the sound.

The children and I ran. Hours later, when we emerged from the woods, the sun was rising.

8

Reunions followed. Halfmoon found his mother, Zel found Bregna, Lommy found Piebald, and Pia found Lara and Lorn. I wished I could've stayed to see it, but I had other matters to attend to.

Exhausted though I was, I led five men back into the Creaking Wood. I was no tracker, but I remembered the way. "Be prepared," I warned them. "It might still be here."

It wasn't. When we entered the clearing, we discovered only a splintered shrine, a broken axe, and a splash of blood in the snow. We searched nearby, but found nothing more.

We returned to Greengrove with a feeling of unease. Should we evacuate the village? Should we prepare to fight this Nameless Prince? And what of Lockwood?

The elements decided for us. An exodus would be impossible in these deep snows, even for our small population. So we had to arm ourselves as best we could. And wait.

I did not sleep that night. I'm sure none of us did. My thoughts jumped between hope that Lockwood would emerge from the woods and fear that the birds would emerge instead. Neither did.

Piebald visited my quarters the following morning. He stared at my feet while he spoke.

"I've made a great many mistakes in my life," he said. "And I hope the Goddess forgives me for them. But for this one, for doubting you and renouncing my trust in you…I only ask for your forgiveness, Wendyll. I'm sorry. I'm so sorry."

Without a moment's hesitation, I said, "I forgive you, Piebald. Don't dwell on it. You and I, we aren't divine. We make mistakes. We're just people." And we embraced.

That afternoon, I stood at the edge of the Creaking Wood. The sun hung above the treeline and the air held unseasonable warmth, yet suddenly, I wept. I wept with relief that we'd found the children and with dread that evil might still linger in the woods. Yet most of all, I wept with sadness that I might never see Lockwood again. I cried and cried and—I stopped. There, in the distance, came the sound of crunching footsteps.

My breath quickened. Something was drawing near, lurching through the trees on unsteady legs. It was a broad, hulking, shambling shape. It limped closer.

"W-w-who goes there?" I stammered.

The figure answered, "Your fucking savior. Do you have any stew, by chance?"

She appeared from the forest and spat blood upon the snow. She bore cuts and gashes and scrapes all over her body and face. Her left side was soaked in blood, though whether it was hers or someone else's, I could not say.

"Nairn Lockwood," I gasped. "You're alive!"

"Not for long if you stand there gawking like that. Move your holy ass, Pureman."

I showed her to my quarters and there spent several hours administering poultices, bandages, and restorative potions. The woman screamed all manner of nasty curses and insults, mostly directed at me (the rest were for the Goddess). Still, her wounds had not mortified and she'd made it this far without perishing, despite the severity of the damage. It was as if Lockwood simply refused to die.

"I believe you'll live yet," I said when I was finished. "Just don't pick a fight with any more ancient gods."

"Speaking of which…" She grinned, revealing those missing teeth. "I hope you haven't finished writing my story. I haven't told you the next chapter."

"Tell me everything."

She did. Lockwood described their final battle, first beneath the moon, then beneath the sun as it rose in the morning.

"Very dramatic," she said. "Worthy of one of that silly actor's plays. By the way, he won't be getting that costume back."

According to Lockwood, they dueled ceaselessly. The amalgam that had been Glendon Glubb fought only with the long knife, yet it moved with inhuman speed. Also, according to Lockwood, it felt no pain and showed no signs of fatigue.

"Had to draw it into the forest," she said. "I plunged deeper into the woods, deeper than anyone's likely ever been. Evaded the thing for an entire day, baiting it further and further away from the village. Don't give me that look, Pureman. It wasn't a retreat. Nairn Lockwood *never* retreats."

She'd managed to hide and recover her strength, relying on her inexhaustible supply of food for fresh energy (meat taken from Bregna the Butcher's shop, I understand). And finally, when she returned to battle, she'd simply hacked the thing to pieces.

"It was fast and unaffected by pain, but it couldn't do much without limbs. Eventually the birds scattered and abandoned the remains. I would've returned with the head, only there wasn't much of it left."

"Lockwood," I said. "You saved the children. You saved me. I don't know how I can repay you."

She snapped her eyes shut. "You can repay me by letting me sleep. I'm a tad fatigued."

I smiled. "Very well. I believe you've earned it." I doused the lights and stepped outside.

9

By then darkness had fallen. The moon returned, not much changed from two nights ago. Old snow crunched beneath my boots. My breath swirled about my face.

The Creaking Wood, once so eerie and ominous, now seemed peaceful. It was as if the fear had been drained from it, like bad blood from a wound. How could trees be frightening compared to what I'd seen two nights ago? As if to prove a point to myself, I stepped among them, and within them.

It was like entering another world. The boughs creaked with the wind, the air carried the aroma of leaves and sap. An owl hooted somewhere nearby. I spread my arms as I walked and brushed my fingers over the branches. I stood among it all. I breathed in. Breathed out.

Movement on the edge of my vision. Something large. My mind flicked back to the swarm of birds, but it wasn't them. It couldn't be. Lockwood had slain that thing. Yet whatever it was, it was massive. And certainly not human.

It emerged from the dark and approached me. It walked with peculiar grace for such an immense creature, treading carefully on two featherless legs. Its small wings trembled as though it was shivering. Its black plumage rustled in the breeze. A curved beak opened and shut silently, as if it had something to say, yet couldn't find the right words. Its eyes were old, and droopy, and tired.

The Megrim.

I recognized it from that night in the woods so long ago. That hadn't been a man in a costume and this wasn't, either. Back then I'd felt so small, so profoundly overcome by fear. Now, however, I had a feeling I thought I'd forgotten...

Wonder.

When the Megrim came near, I reached out and touched its beak. The texture was like porcelain. The creature did not seem threatened. It only studied me.

"We've got you all wrong, don't we?" I murmured. "The books, the stories. All wrong."

Those old eyes blinked slowly. They gazed with a depth of intelligence I'd never seen, not before or since. This creature understood things I could never fathom. This creature knew truths I never would.

"I'll tell them," I vowed. "I'll show them."

The Megrim made no sound, yet a ripple of understanding passed between us. Then it turned and paced back into the trees. I never saw it again.

***

10

When I slipped through the door to my quarters, I found Lockwood, already awake.

"Well," she said. "I'm off."

"Off? Off to where? You need rest. *Months* of rest."

"Months, days, hours, minutes. All close enough. Besides, I have money to collect from your High Pureman. So if you'll excuse me..." She gathered her meager belongings, stuffed them into a sack, hoisted it over her shoulder, and exited.

There we stood, Lockwood lingering on the path out of town, me waiting after her.

"So you're leaving us," I said. "For the second time."

She glared at me. "I did come back."

"Will you come back again?"

"I'm a mercenary, Pureman. Impermanence is the price of the job."

I knew this, of course. No mercenary stays anywhere for long. They follow the coins. They don't settle in quaint villages like Greengrove. This I knew. Yet it made our parting no easier.

I offered my hand, the one with the missing fingers. "I've never met anyone like you before, Lockwood, and I suspect I never will again. I'm glad I did."

She considered my hand for a moment. Then she clasped it with hers, the one missing a finger, and shook. "Same, Pureman. If we ever meet again, maybe you could show me how to read one of those books you're so keen on. A cooking book, perhaps." She gave a final wave, then trudged up the path.

When she disappeared over the rise, I turned and regarded Greengrove. The village slept peacefully, bathed in the silvery glow of the moon on high. No more fear of the woods.

My thoughts drifted to the children. I prayed for them to forget the whole ordeal and simply enjoy their youth. They deserved happiness, those four, Halfmoon and Zel and Lommy and Pia.

Pia. My apprentice. The brave girl who ventured into the Creaking Wood to save her fellow townsfolk. The fiery apprentice who could already quote more scripture than ever I could. The eager young woman who wanted more than anything to be a Purewoman.

I re-entered my quarters, the place I'd called home for most of my life. I found a scrap of parchment and wetted my quill, then scratched a brief message. I folded it in half and wrote three words on the outer flap:

For Purewoman Pia.

I stepped out into moonlight. I breathed in the chilly air. And then I set off at a jog.

"Lockwood!" I called. "Wait! You're forgetting something! You're forgetting…your *partner!*"

ACKNOWLEDGMENTS

"Unbelievable" was first published by *Chantwood Magazine* in 2017. Thank you to the editors for giving a story about vampires a chance.

"Thespian: A Tale of Tragedy and Redemption in Three Acts" was first published in 2016 in *Allegory Magazine*. Thank you to Ty and the editors for giving me my first professional publication.

"Wings" was first published in the 2016 edition of *Five on the Fifth*. Thank you to the editors for publishing a story about a demented weirdo and a person who wants to fly.

"Large Coffee, Black" was first published on my blog in 2015. Thanks to coffee for waking me up every morning. May you never go extinct.

Thank you to Nathan Rumsey for designing another knockout cover. I know many readers would never open this book if not for your creativity and generosity.

Thank you to Katheryn, Laura, Sara, Heather, Neal, Geoff, Nathan, and Levi for your always excellent feedback. None of these stories would work without your help. Thanks especially to Katheryn, Laura, and Levi for your invaluable feedback on "The Megrim."

Thank you to Jamie and Sheryl for providing legal insight on "Virus / Affliction / Condition / Curse."

Thank you to ProWritingAid for refining my prose. Try it out yourself at prowritingaid.com.

Thank you to my parents for always supporting me at whatever I do.

Thank you to my wife for being a master inventor and finisher of night projects. Love ya, Sqummy.

ABOUT THE AUTHOR

Kyle A. Massa is a speculative fiction author living somewhere in upstate New York with his wife and their two cats. When he's not writing, he enjoys reading, running, drumming, and daydreaming about playing Magic: The Gathering professionally. You can learn more about Kyle and his work at his website, kyleamassa.com.

Gerald Barkley Rocks

If your life was a song, what would it sound like? In the case of Gerald Barkley, it would be an elevator jingle.

The debut novel from speculative fiction author Kyle A. Massa, *Gerald Barkley Rocks* examines music, fame, mortality, and the strangeness that composes them all. One part detective story, one part rock-and-roll elegy, and one part supernatural comedy, this book might just change your outlook on life—and death.

Past, Present, Future.

Three eras, three stories. A triptych collection that explores fantasy, science fiction, and humor. Free to download from kyleamassa.com.

Made in the USA
Middletown, DE
01 December 2019